Acting Edition

Four Old Broads on the High Seas

by Leslie Kimbell

SAMUEL FRENCH

FOR PRODUCTION INQUIRIES

UNITED STATES AND CANADA
info@concordtheatricals.com
1-866-979-0447

UNITED KINGDOM AND EUROPE
licensing@concordtheatricals.co.uk
020-7054-7298

Each title is subject to availability from Concord Theatricals Corp., depending upon country of performance. Please be aware that *FOUR OLD BROADS ON THE HIGH SEAS* may not be licensed by Concord Theatricals Corp. in your territory. Professional and amateur producers should contact the nearest Concord Theatricals Corp. office or licensing partner to verify availability.

No one shall make any changes in this title(s) for the purpose of production. No part of this book may be reproduced, stored in a retrieval system, scanned, uploaded, or transmitted in any form, by any means, now known or yet to be invented, including mechanical, electronic, digital, photocopying, recording, videotaping, or otherwise, without the prior written permission of the publisher. No one shall share this title(s), or any part of this title(s), through any social media or file hosting websites.

For all inquiries regarding motion picture, television, online/digital and other media rights, please contact Concord Theatricals Corp.

MUSIC AND THIRD-PARTY MATERIALS USE NOTE

Licensees are solely responsible for obtaining formal written permission from copyright owners to use copyrighted music and/or other copyrighted third-party materials (e.g. artworks, logos) in the performance of this play and are strongly cautioned to do so. If no such permission is obtained by the licensee, then the licensee must use only original music and materials that the licensee owns and controls. Licensees are solely responsible and liable for clearances of all third-party copyrighted materials, including without limitation music, and shall indemnify the copyright owners of the play(s) and their licensing agent, Concord Theatricals Corp., against any costs, expenses, losses and liabilities arising from the use of such copyrighted third-party materials by licensees. For music, please contact the appropriate music licensing authority in your territory for the rights to any incidental music.

IMPORTANT BILLING AND CREDIT REQUIREMENTS

If you have obtained performance rights to this title, please refer to your licensing agreement for important billing and credit requirements.

FOUR OLD BROADS ON THE HIGH SEAS received its World Premiere Production at Winder Barrow Community Theatre in Winder, Georgia on March 1, 2019. It was directed by Léland Downs Karas and assistant director Samantha Webb. The scenic design was by Leslie Kimbell and Léland Downs Karas. The lighting and sound were done by Pamela Veader. Costume design was by Eddie Nadeau. Graphic design work by Larry Germain. The cast was as follows:

BEATRICE SHELTON............................Billie Nye-Muller

EADDY MAE CLAYTON.............................Elinor Hasty

IMOGENE FLETCHER..................................Linda Keller

MAUDE JENKINS...........................Linda Moore Oulton

SAM SMITH.......................................Thomas Manley

HERBERT...Scott Jones

CAPTAIN SHELDON STERLING.........................Ken Greene

STEVEN DUPREE/TEQUILA MOCKINGBIRD...........Tony Smithey

JIM ROCKSTONE/MELVIN TRICKLE......................Klo Lopes

HORACE BUMPUS......................................Rick Jarvis

EDNA BUMPUS.......................................Peggy Marx

The World Premiere Production was dedicated in loving memory of Patricia Ann Kimbell - mother-in-law, best friend and the wind beneath my wings

CHARACTERS

BEATRICE SHELTON – Senior, bawdy former burlesque dancer

EADDY MAE CLAYTON – Senior, desperately religious

SAM SMITH – Senior, former Elvis Impersonator and fiancée to Imogene

IMOGENE FLETCHER – Senior, sassy and bold fiancée of Sam

MAUDE JENKINS – Senior, dingbat wannabe beauty queen

HERBERT – Fifties/sixties, Slick and overly tan villain

CAPTAIN SHELDON STERLING – Fifties/sixties, ship's captain

STEVEN DUPREE/MISS TEQUILA MOCKINGBIRD – Twenties/forties, luggage porter by day and drag queen entertainer by night

JIM ROCKSTONE/MELVIN TRICKLE – Thirties/forties, bumbling ship's detective

HORACE BUMPUS – Senior, rickety and browbeaten husband

EDNA BUMPUS – Senior, rickety and hard of hearing wife

SETTING

The Atlantic Queen Cruise Ship. The Main Set is the Starlight Lounge. Other scenes take place in front of the curtain or in a pool of light.

TIME

Spring 1992

AUTHOR'S NOTES

Imogene is: EYE-MO-JEAN

Eaddy is: Ee-dee

Beatrice is: Bee-uh-triss

These characters, while fun and sassy, should be portrayed as vital and real people, not caricatures in any way.

The author suggests that **HERBERT** come out for the curtain call wearing the life preserver around his neck and handcuffs.

STEVEN does not have to be a professional drag queen.

It is my desire to create roles for senior actors, who are often overlooked for theatrical roles. However, the senior roles can be portrayed by any actor with the magic of theatrical makeup.

For Léland
My True Friend. My Heart. My Boom.

ACT I

Scene One

(Tropical Steel Drum Music Intro and the sound of a cruise ship horn.)*

VOICE-OVER. Last and final call for boarding. *The Atlantic Queen* sets sail in one hour. Again...last and final call for boarding. All ashore that are going to shore. To all our valued passengers...we know you have a choice when you travel...and we thank you for choosing Regency Cruise Lines. We hope you all enjoy your Sassy Seniors Cruise. Again...this is last and final call for boarding... all ashore that are going to shore. *(Ship's horn as music fades.)*

> **(BEATRICE, EADDY, IMOGENE,** *and* **MAUDE** *enter wearing tropical travel wear. All the ladies wear floral leis.* **MAUDE** *is wearing a MISS MAGNOLIA SENIOR CITIZEN sash and a rhinestone crown. Behind them we see a sign with the name of the ship; THE ATLANTIC QUEEN.)*

BEATRICE. I cannot believe that we almost missed boarding. We left at six this morning.

---

* A license to produce *Four Old Broads On The High Seas* does not include a performance license for any third-party or copyrighted music. Licensees should create an original composition or use music in the public domain. For further information, please see the Music and Third-Party Materials Use Note on page iii.

MAUDE. We must have stopped at every Stuckey's and dirty gas station between here and Petula...not that I'm complaining of course... I do love a good pee-can log. *(She takes a bite of a pecan log.)*

IMOGENE. If I've told you once...I've told you a million times...my bladder is the size of a pea.

BEATRICE. Well...*I* told *you* to wear bladder pants.

EADDY. Imogene...I don't want to get into your personal business...but have you seen a doctor about that? You may have a little problem...you know...down there...it that uh...general vicinity. I mean...you have to tinkle every five minutes.

IMOGENE. Yes...of course I did...he couldn't find anything wrong... I'm just old and I have to tinkle a lot.

BEATRICE. Well...I would have taken *my* kitty to a different vet.

EADDY. Beatrice! You are so vile!

(**BEATRICE** *is waving and winking at all the "men" she sees in the distance as she talks.*)

BEATRICE. I'll show you vile...if I don't get my choice of all the eligible men on this ship because of your overactive bladder...there is going to be hell to pay.

IMOGENE. Sorry Beatty –

EADDY. Well...I guess we know what Beatrice will be doing the next nine days –

MAUDE. We may as well strap a mattress to her back.

EADDY. Can't you at least wait until we set sail to start acting like a common heathen?

BEATRICE. *(Sweetly.)* Eaddy...BITE ME!

MAUDE. When I grow up...I want to be just like Beatrice. Everywhere she goes...she picks up a man.

EADDY. Yeah...so do prostitutes.

> (**MAUDE** *pull out her camera and spins around in excitement. She takes a picture using the flash.*)

MAUDE. OOOOO this is so glamourous... I'll bet this is how they felt boarding...the *Titanic*.

IMOGENE. That is *not* a comforting cruise ship reference!

BEATRICE. Maude...when are you going to take that stupid crown and sash off...you look ridiculous.

EADDY. Oh, leave her alone Beatrice...she's proud she won the Miss Magnolia Senior Citizen pageant. Let her have her moment.

MAUDE. Don't be jealous Beatrice. Remember...we can't all be queen...I need someone to clap as I walk by...it may as well be you.

> (**SAM** *enters wearing a Hawaiian shirt, shorts, dark socks and white loafers. He is loaded down with luggage and is openly straining under the weight.*)

SAM. Ladies...I think my knees are breaking. What did you pack in here?

IMOGENE. Oh, here sweetie...let me help you.

> (**IMOGENE** *grabs* **BEATRICE**'s *bag from* **SAM.***)

BEATRICE. No no no wait...be careful...that's my bag and the zipper is –

> (*The bag falls open and several pieces of tacky lingerie, a tassel whip, paddle, handcuffs, feather duster and other funny and sexy items fall out.* **EADDY** *holds up a comical large sized negligee with attached pasties and then looks at* **BEATRICE** *with disgust.* **MAUDE** *takes a picture using the flash.*)

SAM. *(Looking down.)* What the hell is that?

MAUDE. *(Pointing to the ground.)* Is that handcuffs?

BEATRICE. *(Indignant.)* WHAT? When are y'all gonna get used to me?

EADDY. This is a scrap of cheap chiffon and a piece of elastic. I mean...I don't want to get into your personal business...but why bother wearing anything at all?

BEATRICE. I don't wear it very long...trust me.

> (**SAM** *holds up a small box and squints at the words on the box.)*

SAM. Does this say *edible* underwear?

MAUDE, EADDY & IMOGENE. Edible underwear?

> (**SAM** *holds the box out for the others to see.* **EADDY** *gasps.* **MAUDE** *takes a picture using the flash.)*

EADDY. I think we need to pray... Dear Lord...please forgive this heathen Jezebel...and please forgive me for continuing to associate with her...as I am weak and easily misled. Please do not send down a bolt of lightning to destroy the ship...or a plague of boils or locusts...or hemorrhoids...AMEN.

BEATRICE. Thank you Eaddy. I hope that will conclude the fire and brimstone portion of our trip. Now give me that.

> (**BEATRICE** *snatches the negligee and box away.)*

EADDY. RUDE!

BEATRICE. PRUDE!

EADDY. WITCH!

BEATRICE. BITCH!

(They embrace.)

BEATRICE. I love ya...ya old Bible Thumper.

EADDY. I love you too...Mary Magdalene.

IMOGENE. Hey Beatrice...do you have anything in your little bag of tricks that I can borrow for our honeymoon?

*(**IMOGENE** picks up a feather duster.)*

What in the world do you do with this?

BEATRICE. Use your imagination –

EADDY. Beatrice...you really are a pervert.

BEATRICE. I AM NOT! I'm just kinky. Kinky is when you use a feather duster...*perverted i*s when you use the whole chicken.

*(**SAM** picks up the items and puts them back in the bag. **IMOGENE** takes a tassel whip and swats his bottom.)*

SAM. Hubba Hubba.

BEATRICE. HEY...get your own!

*(**BEATRICE** snatches the whip. Unnoticed, **IMOGENE** sneaks a pair of handcuffs into her purse.)*

IMOGENE. Selfish!

*(Enter **CAPTAIN SHELDON STERLING**, a handsome man in his sixties. He wears a captain's shirt with nametag and navy shorts as well as his captain's hat. He has a two-way radio on his belt. All the ladies...especially **BEATRICE** are immediately mesmerized.)*

CAPTAIN. Welcome aboard ladies...oh *and* gentleman. I'm so glad you made it. Five more minutes and you would have missed boarding.

> (**EADDY** *steps forward.* **MAUDE** *takes a picture using the flash.*)

EADDY. Well thank you Captain *(She squints to read his nametag.)* Sterling. It's so nice of you to come and greet us personally.

> (**BEATRICE** *pushes* **EADDY** *out of the way and drapes her arm across the* **CAPTAIN***'s shoulder.*)

BEATRICE. Well, hell-o handsome...I just love a man in uniform. My name is Beatrice...but you can call me... EASY.

> *(She is still holding the tassel whip and lightly fans herself with it. The* **CAPTAIN** *shifts uncomfortably.)*

IMOGENE. That was subtle.

MAUDE. Like a sledgehammer to the neck.

SAM. *(Desperate.)* Excuse me Captain...but is there someone that can take our luggage?

CAPTAIN. Yes...certainly...I'll get you a porter. *(He speaks into his radio.)* This is Captain Sterling; I need a porter to the main gateway entrance...*right away.*

BEATRICE. Oooooo you are so commanding.

> (**MAUDE** *steps forward and extends her hand.)*

MAUDE. I'm not sure if you noticed my crown and sash... but I just won the Miss Magnolia *Beauty* Pageant yesterday. I'm a real beauty queen.

       (**MAUDE** *steps in and takes a "selfie" with the*
       CAPTAIN, *using the flash. He winces.*)

CAPTAIN. I see that...and don't you look lovely. Miss Magnolia?

BEATRICE. *(Big angry smile.)* It's just a little thing they do at our...uh...little community.

MAUDE. We live in an assisted living facility in Petula, Georgia. It's called Magnolia Place.

BEATRICE. *(Gritted smile.)* Maude sweetheart...unless you want to *eat* that crown for dinner... I suggest you back off.

IMOGENE. I'd listen to her Maude...if you value your teeth.

CAPTAIN. Yes...well ladies...oh *and* gentleman...as Regency Cruise line VIP guests...I would like to invite you to a private cocktail reception as we set sail...in the Captain's Lounge by the bridge.

BEATRICE. *(Sensuous.)* I don't know about you girls...but I could certainly use a nibble.

EADDY. Yes Beatrice...you should definitely go and have a...*Whore*-derv.

       (**EADDY** *and* **BEATRICE** *make faces at each other.*)

CAPTAIN. Now...I understand I will be marrying someone from this group...once we set sail.

SAM & IMOGENE. *(Gushing.)* THAT'S US!

CAPTAIN. Wonderful. Perhaps at the reception we can discuss the details of your ceremony. The bow of the ship is a nice place to have a wedding...or we can always use the ship's chapel if you like.

SAM. I don't care where we have the wedding... I'm just ready to get the honeymoon started.

(SAM and IMOGENE snuggle and peck kiss.)

EADDY. I don't want to get into your personal business... but y'all practically had a honeymoon in the backseat of the Lincoln on the way here.

MAUDE. *(Giggling.)* In my lap most of the time...but I'm not complaining... I just love living vicariously through your romance.

CAPTAIN. Yes...well...once the ship sets sail, we will –

(Enter STEVEN DUPREE, the overtly fabulous porter, pushing a luggage cart. A clipboard hangs from a hook on the cart.)

STEVEN. Hellooo Ladies...oh...*and* gentleman...welcome aboard *The Atlantic Queen*...and when I say queen...I don't mean me!!!

(STEVEN giggles as he begins to take the luggage from SAM when EADDY suddenly recognizes him.)

EADDY. Wait...Steven? Steven Dupree?

STEVEN. Why yes darlin' the one and only...have we met?

EADDY. Yes...yes...I'm Eaddy Mae Clayton. I am...well... we are all...friends with your Grandmother Mable and your Aunt Lurleen. We all live at Magnolia Place Assisted Living in Petula.

STEVEN. Shut up! Small world!

BEATRICE. Hello Steven...how are you?

STEVEN. Hello! Now I *definitely* remember you...*you're* Beatrice...the one that was a stripper back in the old days.

CAPTAIN. *(Wide-eyed.)* A stripper?

EADDY. She was *not* a stripper...she was *(Grandly.)* a Lady of Burlesque...she was Miss Bang Bang La-Dish "The

Best Guns in the West". She could do a striptease...twirl her lasso...*and* swing both of her bullet pasties in two different directions...all at the same time.

CAPTAIN. *(Uneasy.)* Oh...well...hmmm...how about that? *(Unsure.)* Good for you –

BEATRICE. *(She shimmies.)* You have no idea. *(Then to* **STEVEN.***)* I haven't seen you since you performed at The Miss Magnolia Senior Citizen Pageant...what...a year ago?

MAUDE. *(Stepping forward.)* Which...in case you didn't notice... I won this year!

>   (**MAUDE** *steps forward and takes a "selfie" using the flash.* **STEVEN** *squints and blinks.)*

BEATRICE. No one cares Maude...and GIVE ME THAT! *(She snatches the camera. Then.)* So how are you sugar?

STEVEN. Look at me...I'm fabulous. I mean...I do have my Porter duties during the day...but at night I perform in the Starlight Cabaret Lounge on The Promenade Deck...doing my *fabulous* drag act.

CAPTAIN. It's one of the more popular shows on the ship.

MAUDE. Oh, I just *loved* your drag queen act...especially when you did that Barbra Streisand impersonation. *(She begins to belt out an out of tune and not very identifiable song.)* ALL THE... MEEEEEMORIES...of *the rain on a parade...in my mind...and look at all the PEOPLEEEEE...at the puhhhh-raaaddddeee –*

STEVEN. *(Touching* **MAUDE***'s shoulder.)* Oh honey...no...no no NOOOO...don't do that...ever...again...please.

BEATRICE. DEAR GOD MAKE IT STOP!

IMOGENE. Yes...okay...I remember y'all telling me about that drag show. I didn't live at Magnolia Place back then. *(To* **STEVEN.***)* What's your lady name?

STEVEN. *(Fabulous pose.)* When I'm in drag...I'm...Miss Tequila Mockingbird...and I am too fabulous for words. Don't worry...I still do Barbra. I do Marilyn Monroe and Liza Minelli too... I love Liza.

BEATRICE. *(Aside to the others.)* The gays just love their Liza.

STEVEN. I can't wait to tell Nana Mable and Aunt Lurlene I saw you ladies. Now let me get this luggage to your rooms. Last names on the reservation?

BEATRICE. Fletcher and Shelton.

> (**STEVEN** *grabs the clipboard off the luggage cart and checks for their names.*)

STEVEN. Fletcher...Fletcher...OH...the honeymoon suite... Ooo la la. Who's getting married?

SAM & IMOGENE. *(Gushing.)* We are.

> (**BEATRICE** *makes the gagging motion with her finger down her throat.*)

STEVEN. Well follow me and I will show you to your suite. It's quite lovely...it has a spacious balcony...and ladies... I'll take your luggage to your room too...403 on The Plaza Deck.

> (**STEVEN** *loads the luggage.* **SAM** *and* **IMOGENE** *snuggle and giggle like teenagers as they exit...calling back.* **STEVEN** *follows.*)

IMOGENE. Don't call us...

SAM. We'll call you...maybe –

EADDY. Y'ALL STAY OFF THAT BALCONY! *(Then.)* I can see it now...those two are gonna fall buck naked into the ocean. *(Then.)* Dear Lord...please don't let my friends fall into the ocean during the fornication I know they will be doing on that balcony. And please help me as I try to survive this floating Sodom and Gomorrah surrounded by sinners of Biblical proportion and all the – *(Her voice trails as she exits.)*

BEATRICE. Well...hmmmm...that just leaves you Maude.

MAUDE. Leaves me what?

BEATRICE. Leaves you...to...you know...how can I say this nicely...to...um *(Smiling.)* get the hell out of here.

MAUDE. *(Grabbing her camera.)* Nice Beatrice...real nice. So much for winning the Miss Magnolia Pageant. I mean...what does a beauty queen have to do to get a little attention around here. What am I? Chopped liver? I've got the crown and the sash...where's *my* Romeo...where's *my* Prince Charming –

> *(**MAUDE**'s voice trails as she exits. **BEATRICE** strikes a sexy pose.)*

BEATRICE. Now...where were we?

> *(**BEATRICE** swats the **CAPTAIN** with the little whip which makes him uncomfortable.)*

CAPTAIN. Um...I believe I was going to escort you to the reception.

BEATRICE. Or maybe...you could show me your cabin –

> *(The **CAPTAIN** is taken aback by **BEATRICE** boldness.)*

CAPTAIN. Oh...um...I am so sorry... I just remembered I have to...uh...make the departure and safety announcements. I'll uh...see you at the reception.

> *(The **CAPTAIN** hurries off, leaving **BEATRICE** very angry.)*

BEATRICE. Dammitt!

(We hear a man's whistle and cat call. **BEATRICE** *peers into the distance and then smiles as she calls out.)*

BEATRICE. Well, hello handsome...would you like to buy a lonely girl a drink?

(Blackout.)

Scene Two

(Music and the sound of a ship's horn. **MAUDE** *still wearing her crown and sash, stands at the rail of the ship. A sign on the rail indicates that we are on The Lido Deck. She is looking off forlornly into the distance and sadly singing.*)*

MAUDE.
"HERE SHE IS... MISS MAGNOLIA SENIOR CITIZEN... LOOK AT ME... DON'T I LOOK FINE? –" I MEAN C'MON... WHAT DOES A BEAUTY QUEEN HAVE TO DO TO GET A LITTLE ATTENTION AROUND HERE.

(Enter **HERBERT***...a little too slick and overly tan man in his late sixties with a bad toupee... He wears a dated suit and carries two glasses of champagne.)*

HERBERT. Hello there... I hope I'm not disturbing you. But I couldn't help but notice you were here alone. Are you waiting for your husband?

*(***MAUDE** *stares at him blankly, then turns around to see if he is talking to someone behind her.)*

Perhaps a boyfriend...or secret lover?

MAUDE. I'm sorry...are you talking...to me?

HERBERT. Yes, I am beautiful lady –

MAUDE. *(Taken aback.)* Beautiful lady? Me?

---

* A license to produce *Four Old Broads On The High Seas* does not include a performance license for any third-party or copyrighted music. Licensees should create an original composition or use music in the public domain. For further information, please see the Music and Third-Party Materials Use Note on page iii.

HERBERT. I hope I'm not disturbing you?

MAUDE. Oh no...not at all...I was just taking a little stroll and waiting to meet my friends for dinner. You're not disturbing me at all...not at all.

HERBERT. And your husband?

MAUDE. No...I'm not married... I mean I *was* married... oh...but he's dead...dead dead dead...dead as a doornail... I'm just here all by my lonesome...just me, myself and I...doing nothing...and feeling (*Clearing her throat.*)...very thirsty...very parched –

> (**HERBERT** *gives* **MAUDE** *the glass of champagne.*)

HERBERT. Well madame...my name is Herbert...Herbert Vanderbilt.

> (*He grandly takes and kisses her hand.*)

MAUDE. Vanderbilt? As in *Vanderbilt* Vanderbilt?

HERBERT. Yes...well...it's just a name...and I certainly don't want you to feel intimidated.

> (**MAUDE** *giggles nervously and hysterically.*)

MAUDE. Well...it's so nice to make your acquaintance. I'm Maude...Maude Jenkins...the recently crowned Miss Magnolia.

HERBERT. Is that right? Well, I hope I'm not coming on too strong...but I find you very attractive...and I would love to have dinner with you tonight...let's say seven p.m.? I have a beautiful suite on The Promenade Deck...we can have dinner on my private veranda...and get to know each other better. Do you think your friends can live without you for one night?

> (**MAUDE** *giggles hysterically.*)

MAUDE. Friends? What friends?

(**HERBERT** *clinks his glass against* **MAUDE***'s glass.*)

(Blackout.)

Scene Three

> (*Center – In a pool of light...*IMOGENE *and* SAM *are standing at the rail of their private balcony. They are sipping champagne.*)

IMOGENE. This honeymoon suite is gorgeous –

SAM. And look at this view...very romantic –

IMOGENE. Very romantic –

> (*They share a passionate kiss.*)

I can't believe I'm getting married again.

SAM. Are you nervous?

IMOGENE. Yes...a little...but I'm very happy.

SAM. Why nervous sugar pie?

IMOGENE. When I married Bernie...I thought it would be...you know...until death do us part. So, when he ran off with his physical therapist...I didn't think I would ever love anyone again.

SAM. Ah...forget Bernie...let him have that twenty-year-old bimbo...now you have a *real* man...a *strong* man...a *virile* man...OUCH! (SAM *winces in pain and grabs his hip.*)

IMOGENE. Oh sweetie...are you ok?

SAM. Sorry...my hip replacement is acting up...here's a toast to the most beautiful woman in the whole world –

IMOGENE. Oh Sam...now stop –

SAM. I wasn't finished.

IMOGENE. (*Giggles.*) Oops sorry honey...go ahead.

SAM. Here's a toast to the most beautiful woman in the world...a woman who really gets my motor running... (*Beat.*) Raquel Welch.

(**IMOGENE** *acts horrified and then they both giggle.*)

IMOGENE. SAM...stop...get serious now.

SAM. You know I'm kidding... Raquel ain't got nothin' on you baby!

(They peck kiss.)

IMOGENE. Sam...are we doing the right thing? We've only known each other for two weeks...and you've been single all your life...and were quite the ladies man too, according to Beatrice and Eaddy. Are you sure you want to settle down now?

SAM. Yes...I've spent a lot of years drifting from woman to woman to woman *(He has a fond memory.)* to woman... where was I going with this?

IMOGENE. OK I get it Sam...what's your point?

SAM. My point is...the second I saw you I was gaga over you...and I don't want to drift around anymore... you're the one for me sweet cheeks. *(He pops her on the bottom.)*

IMOGENE. Really?

SAM. Yes...really...

IMOGENE. Oh...I can't believe we are doing this.

SAM. I can't either...but I am so happy.

IMOGENE. *(Suggestive.)* Well...I know something that will make you even happier.

SAM. *(Eager.)* Oh yeah?

(**IMOGENE** *reaches into her purse and pulls out a pair of furry handcuffs.*)

IMOGENE. I snuck these when Beatrice wasn't looking... and...I also have these –

> (**IMOGENE** *pulls out a pair of men's red underwear with a Superman symbol on the crotch.*)

SAM. Uh huh...I see...now uh...what exactly are those?

IMOGENE. It's Superman underwear...there's a matching cape too...it's in my suitcase.

SAM. For me? I don't know...I uh–

IMOGENE. OH, c'mon Sam...you know you love it...it'll be fun.

> (**SAM** *takes the underwear and holds them up.*)

SAM. You really want me to wear these...um...*little* things for you?

IMOGENE. Yes...and wait until you see what I'll be wearing.

SAM. *(Wide eyed.)* Oh really...what are you wearing?

IMOGENE. *(Innocently sexy.)* Oops...that's right...I don't have anything to wear...except these – *(She holds up the handcuffs.)*

> (**SAM***'s eyes get large and he smiles with excitement.*)

SAM. Give me two minutes to wrestle myself into these... and I'll be right back.

> (**SAM** *winces in pain...grabs his hip and exits.*)

> *(Blackout.)*

Scene Four

(Music and the sound of a boat horn.[*]* **EADDY** *stands at the rail of the ship. A sign on the rail indicates we are on The Fiesta Deck. She is praying.)*

EADDY. Dear Lord...it's me again...I hope you are not ashamed of me for being here with all these sinners... but mostly...I hope you won't mind...just this once...if I partake in a little of the fun. *(She quickly looks up.)* I just want to try one of those fruity umbrella drinks... and...*maybe* dance with a handsome man. I won't get too carried away...just this once...please? Thank you... AMEN.

*(Enter **HERBERT**...carrying two glasses of champagne.)*

HERBERT. Hello there...I hope I'm not disturbing you. But I couldn't help but notice you were here all alone. Are you waiting for your husband?

*(**EADDY** stares at him blankly and then turns around to see if he is talking to someone behind her.)*

Perhaps a boyfriend...or secret lover?

EADDY. I'm sorry...are you talking...to me?

HERBERT. Yes, I am...beautiful lady –

EADDY. *(Taken aback.)* Beautiful lady? Me?

HERBERT. I hope I'm not disturbing you?

---

[*] A license to produce *Four Old Broads On The High Seas* does not include a performance license for any third-party or copyrighted music. Licensees should create an original composition or use music in the public domain. For further information, please see the Music and Third-Party Materials Use Note on page iii.

EADDY. Oh...uh...no...I was just...uh...waiting to meet my friends for dinner.

HERBERT. And your husband?

EADDY. Yes...I mean no...I'm not married...I mean I was married once...but he died...so...I'm not married anymore...so it's just little 'ole me...just here cruising with my girlfriends... I am *definitely* alone...if that's what you're asking.

> (**HERBERT** *gives* **EADDY** *the glass of champagne.*)

HERBERT. Well, madame...my name is Herbert...Herbert Rockefeller.

> (*He grandly takes and kisses her hand.*)

EADDY. Rockefeller? As in *Rockefeller* Rockefeller? I mean...I don't want to get into your personal –

HERBERT. Yes...well...it's just a name...and I certainly don't want you to feel intimidated.

> (**EADDY** *giggles nervously.*)

EADDY. Well...I'm Eaddy...Eaddy Mae Clayton. It's a *pleasure* to meet you.

HERBERT. I hope I'm not coming on too strong...but I find you very attractive...and I would love to have dinner with you tonight...let's say nine p.m.? I have a beautiful suite on The Promenade Deck...we can have dinner on my private veranda...and get to know each other better. Do you think your friends can live without you for one night?

> (**EADDY** *nods her head and giggles.*)

EADDY. Friends? What friends?

(**HERBERT** *clinks his glass against* **EADDY**'s *glass as she giggles like a school girl.*)

(Blackout.)

Scene Five

(Ships corridor. Elderly couple **HORACE** *and* **EDNA** *shuffle in from stage right. They are dressed very touristy.* **HORACE** *is wearing mismatched plaids and stripes, dark socks, sandals, fanny pack, a large camera around his neck, sun hat and sunglasses.* **EDNA,** *who is pulling her oxygen tank, wears a bright tropical muumuu, excessive jewelry, sunglasses, and a large sun hat. They both have white sunblock on their noses.)*

HORACE. WE HAVE TO GO CHANGE FOR DINNER! HURRY UP EDNA!

EDNA. WHAT?

HORACE. I SAID...HURRY UP EDNA...we're gonna be late for dinner...again. Yap Yap Yap Yap Yap...all you ever do is flap your jaws. You have never been on time in your life.

EDNA. WHAT?

HORACE. I SAID...YOU'RE ALWAYS LATE!

EDNA. A date? OH, how sweet Horace...asking me on date. But don't think you're gonna get lucky tonight.

HORACE. We've been married sixty-four years Edna...and you've had a migraine headache for sixty-two of them. I'm sure not planning on any hanky-panky.

EDNA. CRANKY? Yes... I'm cranky! I'm hungry and I need to take my pills. *(Aside.)* Cranky...that's the pot callin' the kettle black. I can show you cranky!

HORACE. CHECK YOUR HEARING AID EDNA!

EDNA. WHAT?

(**HORACE** *points at his ear dramatically...very irritated.*)

HORACE. Your batteries! CHECK YOUR BATTERIES.

(**EDNA** *adjusts her hearing aid.*)

EDNA. Are we late for dinner?

HORACE. Yes Edna!

EDNA. WHAT DID YOU SAY?

HORACE. I SAID YES...WE ARE LATE!

(**EDNA** *looks at her watch.*)

EDNA. EIGHT? Is it already eight?

HORACE. I SAID WE'RE LATE EDNA...LATE LATE LATE!

EDNA. Well then hurry up and stop all your yapping!

(**CAPTAIN STERLING** *enters stage left.*)

CAPTAIN. Good evening Mr. and Mrs. Bumpus.

HORACE. Good evening Captain Sterling.

EDNA. WHAT DID HE SAY?

HORACE. HE SAID GOOD EVENING EDNA!

EDNA. OH...Good evening Captain.

CAPTAIN. In honor of your anniversary...I have you seated at my table for dinner.

HORACE. Thank you Captain...that's certainly an honor.

EDNA. WHAT DID HE SAY?

HORACE. HE SAID WE ARE SITTING AT HIS TABLE FOR DINNER!

EDNA. A winner? OOOO what did we win?

HORACE.   DINNER...DINNER AT THE CAPTAIN'S TABLE.

CAPTAIN. How long have you two lovebirds been married?

HORACE. Sixty-four years. Sixty-four looooong years.

EDNA. WHAT DID HE SAY?

HORACE. HE ASKED HOW LONG WE'VE BEEN MARRIED!

EDNA. SIXTY-FOUR BLESS-ED YEARS!

(The **CAPTAIN** *gestures for* **HORACE** *and* **EDNA** *to precede him. They cross as they converse.)*

CAPTAIN. Now remind me...where are you two from?

HORACE. We're from Biloxi, Mississippi.

EDNA. WHAT DID HE SAY?

HORACE. HE ASKED WHERE WE'RE FROM!

EDNA. OH...WE'RE FROM MISSISSIPPI!

CAPTAIN. Back when I was at Ole Miss...I went on a blind date with a girl from Biloxi. She was the homeliest and most ignorant girl I have ever met.

EDNA. WHAT DID HE SAY?

HORACE. HE SAYS HE KNOWS YOU!

(Blackout.)

Scene Six

(Tropical music intro and voice-over of **JUDY***...the extra perky cruise director.*)*

FEMALE VOICE-OVER. Good morning cruisers and welcome to another fun-filled day on your sassy senior's cruise. I'm your cruise director Judy...and I want to invite you to join me today for canasta and shuffleboard on The Plaza Deck...or macramé and Bingo in the Sand and Surf Reception Room. We hope you're all ready for the costume party on Friday...it's gonna be *super* fun. Now...don't forget your sunscreen...and remember to stay hydrated. Also...for those of you missing oxygen tanks, walkers, prosthesis, or the like...we have a lost and found room set up by the front desk. We know you have a choice when you travel...and we thank you for choosing Regency Cruise Lines. We hope you are all enjoying your Sassy Seniors Cruise.

(Lights up – **BEATRICE** *and* **MAUDE** *are sitting in two of the four deck chairs.* **IMOGENE** *is pacing nervously. They are wearing bathing suits, caftans, cover ups, hats, sandals and sunglasses...the each have a cocktail with a little umbrella.* **BEATRICE** *is looking through binoculars.)*

BEATRICE. Sassy cruise my ass! If I wanted to play Bingo or do macramé...I would have stayed home. I need some action. I got so desperate last month...I went over to the state prison for a conjugal visit.

MAUDE. Why did you do that again Beatrice? The last time you went...they told you that you actually have to know someone that is in prison there.

(**BEATRICE** *ignores her.*)

BEATRICE. Um um um...that is one fine lookin' man.

MAUDE. OOOO let me see –

(**MAUDE** *grabs the binoculars that are still around* **BEATRICE***'s neck and peers through them...choking* **BEATRICE***.*)

Oh yeah...that is one gorgeous hunk of a man right there...oh yeah work it daddy –

BEATRICE. Give me those damn things...you are choking me!

MAUDE. Selfish!

BEATRICE. I've already told you...I get first pick of all the eligible men.

MAUDE. We'll see about that –

IMOGENE. Could you girls *please* stop acting like two cats in heat? You're getting on my nerves!

BEATRICE. Fine...whatever...when will Sam be back from the doctor's office? All your pacing is making me nauseous.

IMOGENE. I don't know...oh I feel so bad for not being there with him...but they wouldn't let me in to the doctor's office.

MAUDE. Why won't you tell us what happened?

IMOGENE. It's just so embarrassing...and Sam will kill me if I tell you!

MAUDE. You may as well tell us Ima...you *know* Beatrice is gonna nag the hell out of you until she wears you down.

(**BEATRICE** *nods and shrugs.*)

IMOGENE. OK FINE! But promise me you won't tell Sam. He would just die!

BEATRICE. Yeah...sure...whatever –

(*She goes back to looking into her binoculars... uninterested.*)

IMOGENE. *(Pacing.)* Yeah...ok anyway...well I wanted to do something sexy for Sam...so I got him a pair of Superman underwear and a little red cape to dress up in...and –

MAUDE. *(Gasping, she pulls out a fan.)* Superman underwear...oh Mylanta –

BEATRICE. *(Suddenly interested.)* WAIT! OK wait wait wait...I have to picture this...give me a minute...give me a minute. (**BEATRICE** *closes her eyes, scowls and then snort-laughs.*) OK...OK...go ahead...I can see it...I want to throw up...but I can see it.

IMOGENE. *Anyway*...he was gonna be Superman and I was supposed to be Lois Lane...and he was going to (*Air quotes.*) "rescue me." So, I got Sam to handcuff me to the bed –

MAUDE. *(Fanning herself furiously.)* Handcuffs? Is it me or did it just get *really* hot?

BEATRICE. *(Sharp.)* Hey...do you have my handcuffs? I was looking for those last night.

IMOGENE. Yes...fine...whatever...I'll give them back to you...can I finish?

MAUDE. *(Drooling.)* Oh yes...please go on... I'm sweatin' like a hooker in church.

IMOGENE. So...he handcuffed me to the bed and blindfolded me...and I acted like I had been kidnapped. I said "Help...help someone save me"

MAUDE. *(Furiously fanning.)* I think I might need to lie down.

IMOGENE. So anyway...*that's* apparently when he climbed up on the dresser and I heard him say *"Don't worry Lois I'll save you"* ...you see...he was going to jump off the dresser onto the bed like he was flying *(Beat.)* but the dumb ass apparently slipped and fell and hit his head on the nightstand –

BEATRICE. Oh shit –

IMOGENE. *(Tearful.)* –and knocked himself unconscious.

MAUDE. Oh no –

BEATRICE. What did you do?

IMOGENE. I couldn't do anything! I was handcuffed to the bed and blindfolded...and Sam was apparently on the floor unconscious... I kept calling his name, but he wasn't answering...and *that's*...when the room service person started knocking on the cabin door –

BEATRICE. Room service?

IMOGENE. I had ordered champagne and strawberries.

MAUDE. *(Furiously fanning.)* Oooooo how romantic...

IMOGENE. Anyway...the door was locked...and I kept calling for Sam...and when he didn't answer *(Beat.)* I had no choice but to yell out for help...and the ship's security had to come open the door...

MAUDE. Oh no –

BEATRICE. *(Trying not to laugh)* That's just terrible –

IMOGENE. And there I was...handcuffed, blindfolded and...completely butt naked.

     (**MAUDE** *gasps as* **BEATRICE** *laughs out loud.)*

BEATRICE. You mean they saw...everything?

MAUDE. *(Excited.)* Oh, my lord... I think I just tinkled a little.

IMOGENE. So, they called the ship's doctor and hauled him off...and I haven't seen him since.

> (**EADDY** *enters...she is wearing dark sunglasses, a black dress, black shawl and a black hat.*)

BEATRICE. Good Lord...who died?

EADDY. Don't look at me...don't talk to me... I am an evil sinner.

BEATRICE. Does this have something to do with you being out until after midnight?

EADDY. I *don't* want to talk about it.

IMOGENE. Eaddy was out past midnight?

BEATRICE. OOOOOOOO Eaddy...did you get yourself a little pickle tickle last night?

EADDY. RUDE!

BEATRICE. PRUDE!

EADDY. WITCH!

BEATRICE. BITCH!

> *(Beat.)*

MAUDE. Why would someone tickle Eaddy with a pickle... oh wait... I just got it...ooo... I think I just tinkled again.

EADDY. Just to make it very clear to you all...once we've docked... I am going to go and join the nearest convent.

IMOGENE. But you're Southern Baptist.

EADDY. I'LL CONVERT!

BEATRICE. Eaddy...honey...calm down –

(**EADDY** *throws her arms up and dramatically but sincerely begins to pray.*)

EADDY. Dear Lord...the time has now come for you to cast me...*and all* these vile...evil sinners into the fiery pit of hell...I know that I have been a *bad* girl...a sinner of epic proportions –

BEATRICE. A bad girl? OOOOOO spill all the details...and go slow...it's been a while for me.

IMOGENE. This oughta' be good.

(**IMOGENE** *scoots her chair forward and grabs a cocktail.*)

EADDY. I will not discuss *anything* with you.

BEATRICE. Did you at least let him get to second?

EADDY. Second?

BEATRICE. Second base.

IMOGENE. I never have understood the bases.

BEATRICE. Well, it's easy...first base is French kissing, second base is when he –

EADDY. *(Yelling out.)* I LET HIM TOUCH...MY NINNIES.

BEATRICE. Ninnies? Do you mean your tits?

EADDY. *(Horrified.)* Beatrice...at least say *(Whispers.)* breasts.

(**EADDY** *puts her hand to her chest.*)

BEATRICE. Tits tits tits –

IMOGENE. Thank you Beatrice...a dirty mind is a terrible thing to waste.

(**BEATRICE** *takes* **EADDY**'s *hand.*)

BEATRICE. Eaddy I just love messin' with you...hey... where's your diamond ring? You never take it off.

(**EADDY** *looks at her hand puzzled.*)

EADDY. I have no idea... I must have taken it off this morning when I took the scalding hot shower to wash off all the sin. Oh Beatty...I don't want to turn into a...a...trashy woman of loose morals...like you.

MAUDE. Well *I do*...and guess what...I already have!!! I met a man and got lucky last night.

IMOGENE, EADDY & BEATRICE. WHAT?

MAUDE. Well...I mean...not *that* lucky...we didn't get to the fourth base...but we did dance and smooch a little... *with our tongues.*

IMOGENE. OK...that's gross...

BEATRICE. Well ring-a- ding ding...notify the press...

MAUDE. Hey...just because you've been a hoochie mama since puberty is no reason to take away from my romantic tryst.

BEATRICE. Whatever... I'm bored...I've had enough of this crap...I'm heading up to the topless sun deck. *(Beat.)* Y'all like my hot pink thong?

(**BEATRICE** *turns upstage and throws open her robe.* **EADDY** *gasps in horror,* **IMOGENE** *screams and throws her hands out and* **MAUDE** *covers her eyes gagging.*)

EADDY. BEATRICE! Cover yourself up –

(**EADDY** *pulls* **BEATRICE***'s robe closed.*)

MAUDE. Some things can never be unseen.

IMOGENE. Someone please pour bleach in my eyes.

BEATRICE. It's just *(Snarky whisper.)* ninnies.

MAUDE. Ya know...this reminds me of that song.

IMOGENE. What song.

MAUDE. *(She begins to sing.)*
DO YOUR BOOBS HANG LOW... DO THEY WOBBLE TO AND
FRO... CAN YOU TIME 'EM IN A KNOT... CAN YOU TIE 'EM
IN A BOW –

BEATRICE. Shut up Maude...like yours don't hang past
your waist –

EADDY. Beatty, I don't want to get into your personal
business...but what size are those...um...ninnies?

IMOGENE. They looked like about a 34 long to me –

(IMOGENE, EADDY and MAUDE laugh.)

BEATRICE. I'm not saying I hate y'all...but if y'all get run
over by a bus...I'll be the one driving it...bitches –

(They all laugh as BEATRICE. Exits.)

EADDY. Well...I guess I better go up there with Beatty.

IMOGENE. *You're* going to sunbathe topless

EADDY. *(Indignant.) Of course, not*...I would never. These
bosoms haven't seen sunlight since Eisenhower was
President.

MAUDE. Then why are you going?

EADDY. *Someone* has to pry her boobs out of her armpits,
so she can roll over. *(Beat.)* We'll see y'all tonight for
Steven's show in the Starlight Cabaret...unless I leap
overboard between now and then.

(EADDY exits.)

MAUDE. Well...I guess I'll go down to the spa. I want to go
try a bikini wax...you know...just in case.

IMOGENE. I certainly hope they have *a lot* of wax...*and* a blindfold for the waxing lady.

> (**MAUDE** *exits as* **SAM** *enters wearing a head bandage and eye patch. He has on a hospital robe.*)

MAUDE. Sam...thank goodness! Imogene has been worried to death...well excuse me... I'm just going to get a bikini wax –

SAM. Gee Maude...thanks for that visual –

IMOGENE. Oh Sam...I've been worried half to death.

SAM. I need to sit down –

IMOGENE. Are you OK? You look terrible.

SAM. That was the worst experience of my life.

IMOGENE. You poor thing...what happened.

SAM. Apparently that underwear you got me was so tight that it cut off my circulation...so when I climbed up on the dresser...I got dizzy...passed out...and fell and hit my head.

IMOGENE. Oh Sam...what about your eye?

SAM. Well...they tried to pry that underwear off with this thing that looked kinda' like a shoehorn...but they ended up having to cut it off...and the elastic popped up and hit me in the eye...and now I have to wear this thing til tomorrow.

IMOGENE. OH sweetie...what can I do?

SAM. I think you have done quite enough...but thank you.

IMOGENE. What do you mean Sam?

SAM. I mean...I think I may need to reconsider this... *relationship*. You're gonna kill me if I try to keep this up.

IMOGENE. Sam...don't say that. I was just –

SAM. I'm going back to the room to lay down...ALONE!

(**SAM** *exits.*)

IMOGENE. Sam!

(*Blackout.*)

Scene Seven

(Lights up on **HERBERT** *standing at the rail of The Fiesta Deck. He smiles admiringly as he checks his reflection in a pocket mirror and adjusts his toupee. He applies lip balm and then makes a kissing face...then slips the mirror and balm into the breast pocket of his jacket.* **HORACE** *and* **EDNA** *enter left dressed for a formal dinner and slowly cross right.)*

HORACE. It's awfully windy out here on the deck Edna. You should have brought a sweater.

EDNA. WHAT?

HORACE. I SAID...IT'S WINDY OUT HERE ON THE DECK...YOU NEED A SWEATER.

EDNA. WHAT? Speak up Horace...speak up!

HORACE. I SAID...IT'S WINDY...WIIIN-DEEE!!!

EDNA. No it's not...it's Saturday...and I'm cold...you need to go get me a sweater.

HORACE. *(Looking up.)* Take me now Lord...take me now...I'm ready.

EDNA. WHAT DID YOU SAY?

HORACE. *(Very loud.)* NEVERMIND EDNA!

EDNA. *(Huffy.)* WELL...YOU DON'T HAVE TO YELL HORACE.

*(***HORACE** *and* **EDNA** *exit right.* **HERBERT** *snickers and then sprays his breath with breath spray.* **EADDY** *enters left. She is wearing a black evening gown and very sparkly and dangling clip-on earrings. When she sees* **HERBERT,** *she gasps loudly and turns to exit.* **HERBERT** *stops her...grabbing her hand and pulling it to his lips.)*

HERBERT. Where are you going in such a hurry...lovely mademoiselle?

EADDY. OH...hello Herbert...I...I...um...didn't expect to see you tonight.

HERBERT. You look beautiful tonight Elaine.

EADDY. It's Eaddy.

HERBERT. Yes...Eaddy...that's what I said.

(**EADDY** *pulls her hand away.*)

EADDY. Herbert...I...uh...

(**HERBERT** *puts his finger over her lips.*)

HERBERT. There's no need to say anything...beautiful Estelle.

EADDY. Eaddy

HERBERT. Yes...Eaddy...let's just stand here in the moonlight and make love...with our eyes.

(**HERBERT** *stares deeply into her eyes...and places his hand on the side of her face.* **EADDY** *is momentarily mesmerized and then pulls back. As she pulls away...***HERBERT** *slips off one of her earrings and pockets it.*)

What is it my love...why do you pull away? What about our beautiful night together last night?

(**EADDY** *quickly covers her chest for protection.*)

EADDY. I...I'm just...just...not...I...don't normally...do that sort of thing Herbert...I'm not that kind of girl. Oh... I'm so ashamed...I –

(**EADDY** *turns away.* **HERBERT** *turns her back so that her other earring is seen by the* *audience. He places his hand on her cheek and caresses her face.)*

HERBERT. Ashamed? What do you mean my love? Do you mean you are denying our attraction for one another... our hot...passionate...attraction?

*(**HERBERT** slides his hand to her ear and slides off the other earring. **EADDY** is hypnotized... and leans in with her lips quivering and her eyes closed.)*

EADDY. Oh...oh...Herbert.

*(**HERBERT** sees something off in the distance and panic registers on his face. **EADDY** goes in for a kiss, but **HERBERT** steps aside...causing **EADDY** to stagger forward. **HERBERT** turns to her and grabs her shoulders.)*

HERBERT. You must go my love...my beautiful Ethel –

EADDY. *(Irritated.)* It's Eaddy...EADDY!

*(**HERBERT** pulls **EADDY** close.)*

HERBERT. Yes...Eaddy...Eaddy Eaddy Eaddy...beautiful Eaddy...I am so overcome with passion...I don't think I can control my desire for you. *(Beat.)* You must go for now...but I will find you my love...I will find you...now go...go!

EADDY. Oh...well...I –

*(**HERBERT** dramatically twirls **EADDY** right... causing her to fly off right. He holds up the earring and smiles fiendishly...then pockets the earring and smoothly turns to **MAUDE** as she enters left. She is wearing a tacky sequin evening ensemble and a flashy "diamond" bracelet. **HERBERT** grabs her hand and pulls it to his lips.)*

HERBERT. Where are you going in such a hurry...my lovely mademoiselle?

> (**HERBERT** *grabs her hand and pulls it to his lips and kisses up her arm.* **MAUDE** *throws her head back and closes her eyes in ecstasy.*)

MAUDE. *(Giggling.)* Oh...Herbert –

> (**HERBERT** *slips the bracelet off her arm and holds it up into the light...smiling fiendishly... he slips it into his pocket.*)
>
> *(Blackout.)*

Scene Eight

(Lights up. A peppy song plays. A sign reading "Starlight Cabaret Lounge" hangs stage left. **STEVEN** dressed as Miss Tequila Mockingbird, impersonating Barbra Streisand, stands on a small platform stage up center. She is lip syncing to the upbeat song which is playing the final chorus. A disco light twinkles. The rest of the lounge is decorated 1990's. There are silver mylar shimmer curtains on the back of the stage. Three small cocktail tables with two chairs each are scattered about. There are two cased openings on either side of the room. The stage left doorway is the lounge entrance and the stage right doorway leads to the restrooms. A cocktail bar sits up right with the ship's logo on the front. There are bottles of champagne and glasses ready. **EADDY** is seated at a table stage left. She has added a black shawl, black hat and dark sunglasses to her evening ensemble. **MAUDE** stands at the bar and takes a picture using the flash. **STEVEN** winces. The lights suddenly flicker and there is the buzz of a power surge. The stage lights and music go out. The ladies clap lightly...confused.)*

STEVEN. Thank you everyone...thank you so so much...you are too too kind. I am so sorry...it seems we've had a small glitch with the sound and lights. Don't worry... we're not sinking...ha ha ha. I will be back after a short break to bring you another glamourous illusion...of the legend...the goddess...the blonde bombshell...Miss Marilyn Monroe.

---

* A license to produce *Four Old Broads On The High Seas* does not include a performance license for any third-party or copyrighted music. Licensees should create an original composition or use music in the public domain. For further information, please see the Music and Third-Party Materials Use Note on page iii.

> *(STEVEN bows, eagerly awaiting applause...*
> *that never comes. He scowls and exits through*
> *the mylar curtain as* **MAUDE** *crosses to*
> **EADDY.** **MAUDE***'s walk is more of a waddle.)*

MAUDE. This place is dead...and is it just me or does he not look *a thing* at *all* like Barbra Streisand?

EADDY. Yes...it's dead...just like my dirty, dirty, sinful soul...dead and black...and you're right...he looks more like Milton Berle trying to be Eleanor Roosevelt in bad drag. *(Beat.)* Maude, why are you waddling around like that?

MAUDE. I had that bikini wax. They had to use this hot –

EADDY. No...no no...never mind...I don't want to know.

> *(***MAUDE*** does a little squat and shakes her*
> *leg.)*

MAUDE. Ya' know...I'm not one hundred percent sure, but I think they might have accidentally glued my butt together.

EADDY. Please stop talking...and leave me alone to wallow in my self-pity.

MAUDE. Eaddy you are depressing me...and I have a date tonight.

EADDY. A date or a *DAATE*?

MAUDE. What?

EADDY. Listen...I don't want to get into your personal business...but...

MAUDE. But you're going to anyway...right?

EADDY. Yes...well...how should I...I mean...have you had... um...you know...*relations*...since Clarence died?

MAUDE. Relations?

EADDY. You know *(She gestures.) relations.* Oh...don't make me say it –

MAUDE. *(Loudly.)* Are you talking about SEX?

(**EADDY** *Leaps to her feet and begins to pray.*)

EADDY. Dear Lord...please just take a moment out of your busy schedule up there of turning water into wine and healing the lepers...to sink this floating den of iniquity to the bottom of the ocean...I'm ready...it's my time... I've been a terrible terrible –

(*Enter* **BEATRICE** *and* **IMOGENE,** *wearing evening wear.* **BEATRICE** *is very trashy in a high slit gold gown.*)

BEATRICE. A terrible what...friend? I asked you to wait for me while I was looking for my earrings.

MAUDE. What earrings?

BEATRICE. *(Irritated.)* My dangly diamond earrings.

EADDY. Oh yes...I'm sorry...I borrowed them...I'm wearing them –

BEATRICE. No, you're not –

(**EADDY** *reaches up and touches her ears...and then looks puzzled.*)

EADDY. Well...that's strange... I could have sworn I put them on.

BEATRICE. Well, this is the limit...why are you borrowing my things without asking?

EADDY. Well, I –

MAUDE. You know...speaking of jewelry... I can't find my diamond bracelet. Has anyone seen it?

EADDY. You were wearing it last night –

MAUDE. I was? Hmmm...really?

BEATRICE. So, wait...we are missing a ring, a bracelet *and* my earrings? OK ...we need to tell the captain or security...sounds like we may have a kleptomaniac maid.

(**IMOGENE** *enters wearing evening wear.*)

IMOGENE. What we *need* to do is call the ships security about that dress you're wearing...it has *got* to be a crime.

BEATRICE. What? Who put that stick up your butt Ima?

IMOGENE. Excuse me?

EADDY. I *think* she meant to ask why you are in such a bad mood.

(**IMOGENE** *collapses into a chair and begins to sob.*)

IMOGENE. Oh girls...Sam dumped me!

EADDY, BEATRICE & IMOGENE. Dumped you/What?/No!

IMOGENE. He says that I am killing him with my... insatiableness.

EADDY. Your what?

BEATRICE. Killing him with your *insatiableness*? That is a total crock...that man has bedded every woman at Magnolia Place Assisted Living –

EADDY. Except the three of us, of course.

(**BEATRICE** *makes an obvious gesture and look of guilt.*)

BEATRICE. Yes...I mean no...*definitely not one of us.*

IMOGENE. Don't say that...

EADDY. Well, it's true. It's no secret that he has single-handedly kept the Viagra corporation in business.

MAUDE. *(Sweet and gentle.)* What we are trying to say sweetie is...Sam is a whore...a man whore.

IMOGENE. STOP IT! You are talking about the man I love! I knew about Sam's past before I asked him to marry me.

BEATRICE. And yet...you asked him to marry you anyway.

EADDY. Ima...I don't mean to get into your personal business...but...with Sam's reputation...aren't you worried he might be off right now with some other woman.

BEATRICE. Eaddy!

EADDY. Welllll...we are on a boat full of geriatric floozies.

IMOGENE. Oh, I highly doubt that's gonna happen... I dumped all his Viagra overboard.

EADDY. You did what?

BEATRICE. *(Laughing.)* Now that's great! You get more like me every day!

MAUDE. *(Simple.)* Oh Lord...somewhere out there is a really horny octopus.

> (**SAM** *enters...wearing a dinner jacket with his head bandage and eye patch. He crosses to* **IMOGENE.**)

SAM. There you are... I've been lookin' all over...

IMOGENE. Oh Sam...I knew you'd come back.

SAM. What are you talkin' about?

IMOGENE. *(Gushing.)* I knew you still wanted to marry me.

(**IMOGENE** *rushes to throw her arms around*
SAM. *He stops her.*)

SAM. Actually, I just came to tell you that I am getting off
the ship at the next port and going home.

IMOGENE. You're what?

SAM. I didn't want you to think I fell off the ship...so...
well...anyway...goodbye.

IMOGENE. SAM!

BEATRICE. Smooth move Sam...real classy.

MAUDE. *(Rising.)* Well, this is certainly shaping up to be a
fun evening...if you'll excuse me though...I think I am
going to go find Herbert and see if I can at least make it
to the third base before we dock in Montego Bay.

BEATRICE, IMOGENE & EADDY. HERBERT!?

EADDY. Are you talking about Herbert Rockefeller?

MAUDE. *No*...Herbert Vanderbilt.

EADDY. Vanderbilt?

IMOGENE. Wait...a Herbert *Biltmore* made a pass at me
not ten minutes ago out in the hall –

SAM. *(Angry.)* What...made a pass at you?

IMOGENE. Jealous?

SAM. No...I am not.

BEATRICE. *(Suspicious.)* Hmmm...odd...I met a Herbert
Ashcroft this afternoon...and he asked me to dinner
tonight.

(*They all stare at each other for a beat.*)

MAUDE. Wow...there sure are a lot of Herbert's on the ship.

(*Everyone turns and stares at **MAUDE**.*)

BEATRICE.　Maude sweetie...bless your heart...you are as dumb as a box of rocks.

MAUDE.　What?

SAM.　Who is this Herbert? I think I might need to take a crack at him.

IMOGENE.　Oh Sam...you *are* jealous.

SAM.　What? No! I just –

EADDY.　So, wait...Herbert...has been...with you...and... kissing you...and...he touched my...and he touched your... OH GOD I need a drink!

> (**EADDY** *runs to the bar and picks up a champagne glass, looks at, then tosses it aside. She then chugs straight from the bottle as* **CAPTAIN STERLING** *enters from stage right wearing his dress uniform.*)

CAPTAIN.　Good evening everyone...I hope you're all enjoying yourselves.

BEATRICE.　*(Sarcastic.)* Oh yea...it's like Mardi Gras in here...I can't *stand* any more fun.

CAPTAIN.　The second show usually has a much bigger crowd.

MAUDE.　Well, *I'm* not having fun... I just found out that my date is a gigolo.

CAPTAIN.　Yes...well...the show is about to start...do you mind if I join you Miss Jenkins?

MAUDE.　*(Flattered.)* Oh, well...I –

BEATRICE.　Of course, not Captain...please...sit here –

> (*The* **CAPTAIN** *tries to sit by* **MAUDE,** *but* **BEATRICE** *pushes everyone out of her way to sit next to him. There is a drum roll and a fanfare. We hear a voice-over of* **STEVEN** *announcing himself.*)

STEVEN VOICE-OVER. The Starlight Cabaret is proud to present your hostess and emcee for the evening...Miss Tequila Mockingbird.

> *(The main lights lower as the disco lights come on.* **STEVEN** *in drag as Marilyn Monroe comes through the curtain as a lip-sync appropriate song begins.*)*

STEVEN. Good evening everyone...I love you...and this... is...Marilyn –

> *(***STEVEN*** *begins to lip-sync briefly when suddenly, the lights flicker and go out along with the music. In the darkness we hear a gunshot, a scream, breaking glass, and a loud thud. The lights come back on.* **CAPTAIN STERLING** *is on the floor.* **BEATRICE** *jumps from her seat.* **STEVEN** *and the ladies all scream.* **MAUDE** *dramatically faints.* **IMOGENE** *and* **BEATRICE** *catch her.* **STEVEN** *crosses to check* **CAPTAIN STERLING***'s pulse.)*

Oh my God! He's...he's dead!

IMOGENE, EADDY & BEATRICE. Dead? /What?/Holy Shit!

STEVEN. The Captain has been shot.

IMOGENE. Shot?

STEVEN. In the head.

MAUDE. Wait...*DEAD*? Did you say *dead*?

STEVEN. Yes...he's dead...he's been shot in the head...that is what I said –

(**EADDY** *takes another chug of champagne and then throws her hands up.* **STEVEN** *crosses to the bar and pulls up a corded telephone handset and turns away as he "speaks" into it.*)

EADDY. *(Loud.)* AND YEA THOUGH I WALK THROUGH THE VALLEY OF THE SHADOW OF DEATH...I WILL FEAR NO EVIL...

SAM & IMOGENE. Shut up Eaddy!!!!

BEATRICE. This can't be happening.

MAUDE. I want to go home.

EADDY. I put *one* toe over the line...*ONE TOE*...and this is what happens.

STEVEN. Everyone remain calm...I have called ship's security.

MAUDE. REMAIN CALM? There is a dead man with a hole in his head...right there!

EADDY. Who would have done this?

IMOGENE. Are we safe? OH Sam...protect me!

(**IMOGENE** *grabs* **SAM** *and pulls him close.*)

SAM. Well...OK...but just until the police get here.

BEATRICE. I can't believe this.

EADDY. I know...this is awful...just awful...Captain Sterling was –

BEATRICE. ...the one eligible man on the boat that didn't look like Captain Kangaroo...and now he's dead.

EADDY. Tramp –

STEVEN. Who was sitting near him?

(**EVERYONE** *points at* **BEATRICE.**)

BEATRICE. *(Taken aback.)* Well...yes...I was...

STEVEN. Did you hear or see anything when the lights
went out?

BEATRICE. No...I mean...I heard the gunshot and a scream.

STEVEN. That was me screaming –

MAUDE. You scream like a girl.

STEVEN. Oh...thank you...I try –

(**SAM** *crosses to the body and looks down.*)

SAM. Is that a gun?

(**EVERYONE** *gasps and crowds around the
body. They all bend down to look in unison.*)

EADDY. That *is* a gun.

STEVEN. That is a big ole' gun.

MAUDE. Do you think that could be the murder weapon?

(**EVERYONE** *shifts their gaze to* **MAUDE**.
BEATRICE *takes* **MAUDE**'s *hand and pats it
gently.*)

BEATRICE. The wheel's spinning...but the hamster is dead.
Bless your heart –

SAM. Maybe we should get the gun...to keep it safe.

(**SAM** *leans down to get the gun.*)

IMOGENE. NO! Don't touch it! Fingerprints!!!

SAM. Good thinking babe...*I mean*...Imogene.

BEATRICE. Oh hell...this is ridiculous!

(**BEATRICE** *grabs a napkin and picks up the
gun.*)

MAUDE. Wait...how do we know *you're* not the killer?

STEVEN. Oh Lord she's gonna kill us all.

BEATRICE. I'm *a lot* of things...but a killer is not one of them.

EADDY. Yeah...a lot of things...like a Bimbo –

IMOGENE. ...Rude...Hateful –

SAM. ...Self-centered...Conceited...Crabby... Condescending–

BEATRICE. OK OK ...but I'm not a killer.

MAUDE. Well...you *have* been all over the Captain since we boarded the ship. *In fact,* I saw you with him not an hour ago out in the hall.

EADDY. *(Remembering.)* Yeah...so did I...and it looked like you were arguing.

BEATRICE. Yes...that's true...but we were not arguing...just talking. He was telling me that...well...he was telling me that...he's not interested in me.

SAM. Uh – oh.

MAUDE. And so, the plot thickens.

> (**MAUDE** *takes a picture of* **BEATRICE** *using the flash.)*

BEATRICE. Plot? What plot?

STEVEN. *(Dramatic.)* I want to live.

MAUDE. Hell, hath no fury...like a woman scorned.

IMOGENE.	**EADDY.**
Oh Beatrice...what have you done?	Oh Beatty...how could you?

> (**EVERYONE** *stares at* **BEATRICE.**)

BEATRICE. What? So the captain's not interested...that doesn't mean –

MAUDE. *(Bad British accent.)* Is that why you shot him?

BEATRICE. What?

MAUDE. *(Bad British accent.)* I believe we have found our MURDERESS ...y'all!

BEATRICE. MURDERESS? What is this accent? Who are you...Angela Lansbury?

STEVEN. Please don't kill me while I'm wearin' this dress... I hate this dress.

BEATRICE. Are you people crazy? I did not *kill* the Captain!

> (**BEATRICE** *throws her arms up and accidentally fires the gun.* **EVERYONE** *screams and ad libs...help, don't kill me...etc.)*

(Dry.) Well, that was unfortunate.

> *(Enter* **DETECTIVE ROCKSTONE.** *He wears a trench coat and plaid trilby. His gun is drawn.)*

ROCKSTONE. FREEZE! No one touch anything! This is now a crime scene. I am ship's security...Rockstone... Jim Rockstone.

> *(He flashes his badge and drops his gun... then immediately picks it up.)*

What happened here?

> (**EVERYONE** *turns and points at* **BEATRICE.***)*

EVERYONE. SHE DID IT!

> *(Blackout.)*

ACT II

Scene One

(Thirty minutes later. The **CAPTAIN**'s *body has been moved.* **EADDY** *is by the bar drinking. The broken wine glass is still on the bar.* **BEATRICE** *is sitting at the table stage left.* **STEVEN** *has removed his wig and shoes and placed them on the bar. He is pacing on the stage.* **DETECTIVE ROCKSTONE** *stands center. He has an open pad and is writing as he interrogates* **BEATRICE**. **MAUDE** *is down front, pacing and looking through a magnifying glass for clues.* **IMOGENE** *and* **SAM** *are out of sight…behind the bar.)*

ROCKSTONE. Let's go over this again. Tell me again where you were at the time of the murder.

BEATRICE. I've told you a million times…

ROCKSTONE. Tell me again.

BEATRICE. I feel like I'm in *The Twilight Zone* –

> (**MAUDE** *hums something in the style of the*
> Twilight Zone *theme as she peers through her*
> *magnifying glass.*)*

MAUDE. Doo dee doo doo...doo dee doo doo

BEATRICE. *(Calm anger.)* Maude...when this is all over *(Beat.)* there is going to be another murder...and I will confess to that one.

> (**MAUDE** *turns out and holds the magnifying*
> *glass over her eye.)*

MAUDE. So you *are* capable of murder...verrryyy inter-es-ting –

> (**MAUDE** *pulls out a pad and writes on it.*
> **EADDY** *is intoxicated and begins to sing/*
> *hum "Amazing Grace.")*

EADDY.
> AMAZING GRACE – HMM HMM HMMM HMM... THAT SAVED A WRETCH –
>
> *(Sings the following on the same note as "wretch."):*
>
> – (AND EVIL SINNER WHO KNEW BETTER BUT WAS CORRUPTED BY HER HARLOT FRIEND.) LIKE ME!!!
>
> *(Louder.)*
>
> HMMM HMMMM WAS LOST... BUT NOW... *HICCUP* –

BEATRICE. EADDY!

EADDY. Whatever –

---

* A license to produce *Four Old Broads On The High Seas* does not include a performance license for any third-party or copyrighted music. Licensees should create an original composition or use music in the public domain. For further information, please see the Music and Third-Party Materials Use Note on page iii.

(**EADDY** *chugs champagne.* **ROCKSTONE** *crosses to* **STEVEN** *and quietly shows him his notes. We hear* **IMOGENE** *and* **SAM** *giggling behind the bar.)*

IMOGENE. Oh Sam...I'm so glad we made up.

SAM. Me too baby doll

(*A brassiere, sling shots over the bar.* **EADDY** *picks it up, twirls it around and throws it back over the bar.)*

EADDY. Get a room!

(**SAM** *rises from the back of the bar with the bra on his head and lipstick smeared all around his mouth.)*

SAM. *(Pained.)* We would...trust me...but *HE* won't let us leave.

(**SAM** *points at the detective.* **IMOGENE**'s *arm reaches up and pulls him back down.* **STEVEN** *peers behind the bar and is a bit taken aback by what he sees.)*

STEVEN. Oh...oh my...OK now...y'all can't do that in here... y'all are gonna have to...put your clothes back on...and where did you get *THAT*...never mind...I don't want to know...just...just...cover up. *(Gag.)*

ROCKSTONE. Excuse me Mr. Miss Mockingbird Tequila Sunrise...or whoever you are...I have few questions I need to ask you.

STEVEN. Well...I have one first...where did they take the captain's...body?

ROCKSTONE. That information is on a need-to-know basis.

MAUDE. Yeah...only us detectives need to know that stuff. *(Then whispering to* **ROCKSTONE**.*)* So...uh...yeah... where did they take the stiff?

> (**ROCKSTONE** *stares at* **MAUDE** *for a beat... and huffs.)*

ROCKSTONE. Who *are* you exactly?

MAUDE. Maude...Maude Jenkins...beauty queen and amateur sleuth...at your service.

ROCKSTONE. I see...so...Ms. Jenkins...is there anything you remember or can think of that might help us find the murderer?

MAUDE. Oh, I think we have our murderess already, detective.

> (**MAUDE** *gesture to* **BEATRICE**. **BEATRICE** *gives her the bird.)*

ROCKSTONE. Yes...so you say...but do we have irrefutable proof?

MAUDE. Uh...hmm...well... I'm not sure about that *(Beat.)* What does eerie-footable mean?

BEATRICE. Idiot.

MAUDE. Murderer.

ROCKSTONE. Thank you ladies...that is –

STEVEN. I really need to see the captain's body, detective.

ROCKSTONE. May I ask why mam...uh...sir...uh...mister lady?

MAUDE. *(Tough Jersey Cop.)* Yeah...why ya' need to see the stiff?

STEVEN. *(Tearful and nervous.)* I just...well... I'm just –

> (**MAUDE** *peers through her magnifying glass at* **STEVEN**.*)*

MAUDE. Why are you so nervous?

STEVEN. *(Clearly nervous.)* I'm not nervous...why would you ask that...I have no reason to be nervous... I'm not nervous at all.

EADDY. Well, you look nervous to me...and I'm so tanked... I can barely see straight.

BEATRICE. Boy Eaddy...when you let loose...you *really* let loose.

EADDY. Yep...that's me...*hiccup*...I'm just an ole' tee-tootler...tee tottaler...just call me Speedy Eaddy!

STEVEN. *(Dramatic.)* LISTEN! *(Beat.)* I just want to see the captain...because...well...not that it is anyone's business...but...he...he was my lover.

> *(A dramatic DUN DUN DUUUUN organ sound effect plays. **EVERYONE** gasps and then look around to see where the sound came from...including **SAM** and **IMOGENE** who briefly peer over the bar at eye level and then disappear.)*

MAUDE.	EADDY.
Your what?	Your LOVER?

BEATRICE. OH...THANK GOD HE'S GAY!!! I thought I was losin' my touch.

ROCKSTONE. Well, it appears we may have more than one suspect after all.

STEVEN. Wait! Why does being the captain's lover make me a suspect?

BEATRICE. Because he said so...that's why!

ROCKSTONE. And because you are acting very suspicious!

MAUDE. And anyway...everyone knows...it's always the lover...or the butler.

(**EADDY** *reaches over and grabs* **STEVEN**'s *wig from the bar and puts it on. The wig is haphazard and crooked. She reaches out dramatically.*)

EADDY. I'm a pretty girl momma...*hiccup.*

(**STEVEN** *crosses and snatches the wig off her head and puts it on.*)

STEVEN. Excuse me Miss Lady...I don't think so!

(**ROCKSTONE** *is dumbfounded by the idiocy of the scene.*)

ROCKSTONE. *(Shaking his head.)* OK then. *(Beat.)* Now... I think we need to recreate the scene of the crime. I want everyone to return to where they were just before the lights went out. We are going to find out if our killer is our glamourous entertainer...or the provocative Ms. Shelton.

MAUDE. I assume by *provocative*...you mean trashy.

(**EADDY** *bangs on the bar with a champagne bottle.*)

EADDY.   HEY BAMBI...HEY THUMPER...DID YOU HEAR THAT? WE NEED TO...*hiccup*...RECREATE THE SCENE OF THE CRIME! WE NEED TO FIGURE OUT OF IF WAS THE DRAG QUEEN OR THE SLUT!

(**IMOGENE** *and* **SAM** *emerge from behind the bar.* **IMOGENE**'s *outfit is on backwards and her bra is hanging out of her purse.* **SAM** *carries his pants. He is wearing obnoxious heart boxer shorts and socks with garters. They avoid looking at the others.*)

SAM. OK...so...um...we were –

IMOGENE. – over there.

SAM. Excuse us please.

IMOGENE. Thank you.

> (**SAM** *and* **IMOGENE** *cross to where they were as* **BEATRICE** *crosses to her spot.* **SAM** *puts his pants on.*)

BEATRICE. I was over here...BY THE CAPTAIN...which I *have told you fifty hundred times*...and I did *not* shoot him.

MAUDE. Yeah yeah...save it for the jury lady! Call for the paddy wagon Rockstone!

ROCKSTONE. Uh...yeah...the paddy wagon...got it –

EADDY. Well...I was right here...by the bar...and I haven't... *hiccup*...left...not even to go to the bathroom.

ROCKSTONE. Um...thank you...and the rest of you?

> (**STEVEN** *moves to the stage.*)

STEVEN. I was here detective...being fabulous of course.

ROCKSTONE. *(To* **MAUDE.***)* Alright...and where were you Miss Marple?

MAUDE. OK...I was here...and glad to be of help sir.

> (**MAUDE** *crosses to where she was.*)

ROCKSTONE. We have determined the lights were out less than ten seconds. *(He crosses to where the captain was seated.)* OK...I'll be Captain Sterling.

BEATRICE. What is this going to prove?

ROCKSTONE. We are going to try and determine who had the means, motive and opportunity to shoot the captain... I think we already know...this was a crime of passion.

BEATRICE. *(Flirtatious.)* I can certainly show you passion… if you are interested detective.

IMOGENE. *Really* Beatrice? You're gonna do this now?

EADDY. It was Miss Peacock…in the library…with the candlestick…*hiccup*…hee hee hee.

BEATRICE. *(Tearful.)* Listen, detective…just go ahead and arrest me. You all have made up your minds anyway. Don't worry about me…I'm ready for prison… I've seen those women behind bars movies… I'm going to change my name to Cinnamon and get a big strong girlfriend… I'll be fine.

> (**ROCKSTONE** *stares at her for a beat and then continues.*)

ROCKSTONE. As I said…I'll be the captain. Is everyone at the place they were when the lights went out?

> (**EVERYONE** *nods and ad-lib acknowledges that they are in place.*)

Alright…I'm hoping this little exercise will jog someone's memory for other details. Now…I want everyone to close your eyes…and listen for my cue…of the gunshot.

> (**EVERYONE** *closes their eyes.* **EADDY** *hiccups.* **ROCKSTONE** *sits where the captain was and then shouts.*)

BANG!

STEVEN. *Overly dramatic girly scream.)* AHHHHHHHHHHHHHH

MAUDE. OOO…that was very good…I got goosebumps.

STEVEN. Why thank you darlin'…I try –

> (**ROCKSTONE** *lays on the floor.*)

ROCKSTONE. Alright the lights came back on...what happened next?

SAM. Well...I think that's when we all gathered around the body.

IMOGENE. Yes...that's right...and I said, "Oh Sam...please protect me".

> (IMOGENE *is glued to* SAM *as* EVERYONE *moves to their former position around the body.)*

MAUDE. OK...and then the murderess picked up the gun.

BEATRICE. I AM NOT...oh never mind.

SAM. No wait...actually...*I*...was going to pick up the gun... remember?

IMOGENE. Yes...that's right...and I told you not to touch it...in case of fingerprints.

STEVEN. Yes...yes...I remember that –

MAUDE. Then *that's* when the murderess picked up the gun...and tried to kill us all.

> (MAUDE *points at* BEATRICE. ROCKSTONE *stands up.)*

ROCKSTONE. Alright...now...show me where the gun was before the murderess... I mean...suspect got it.

SAM. *(Pointing.)* It was there...to the right of the body.

ROCKSTONE. *(Puzzled.)* To the right?

STEVEN. Yes...right there.

ROCKSTONE. So, it was on the opposite side of the body... from our suspect?

BEATRICE. Who cares? Y'all've already made up your minds about me!

> (**ROCKSTONE** *does a series of wacky moves as he dashes around during his speech... reenacting the crime.*)

ROCKSTONE. So, you were there...and you were there...and *you*...were there...the captain was here...and you were there. THEN...the lights went out...and there was a gunshot...and a scream –

> (**ROCKSTONE** *points at* **STEVEN** *who screams.*)

STEVEN. AHHHHHHHHHH

ROCKSTONE. Then the lights came on...and everyone gathered around the body.

EVERYONE.	EADDY.
Yes./That's right.	*Hiccup.*

BEATRICE. *(To* **ROCKSTONE**.*)* You are so sexy right now –

ROCKSTONE. Then this woman...*cannot* be our murderer –

EVERYONE. Gasp./What?/Why?

> (**MAUDE** *begins to jump up and down and wave her arm in the air.*)

MAUDE. OOO OOO...I know...I know...because the gun was too far away from her. If she had shot the captain and then dropped the gun...the gun would have been to the left of his body and closer to her.

ROCKSTONE. Very good!

BEATRICE. THANK YOU GOD...I'M NOT A MURDERER!

EADDY. You're still a tramp...*hiccup* –

SAM. So who shot him then?

STEVEN. Don't look at me... I'm a sweet southern lady who wouldn't hurt a fly.

MAUDE. So...hmmm...if I was here...and Beatrice was here...and Miss Tequila was there... Ima and Sam were there...and Eaddy was...uh oh –

(EVERYONE *slowly turns their heads to* EADDY.)

EADDY. What...*hiccup*...why is everyone looking at me?

MAUDE. Because...oh Eaddy...you were –

STEVEN. WAIT...I just remembered something. After the gunshot... I heard glass breaking.

EVERYONE. Oh yeah./I remember that./You're right.

(EADDY *slowly rises from the bar.*)

EADDY. Well well well...you think you're clever don't you?

IMOGENE. Oh Eaddy...what did you do?

EADDY. *(Mocking.)* What did you do? *(Beat.)* Yeah...you figured it out...that was me knocking over a glass at the bar...after I pulled the trigger.

MAUDE. I KNEW IT!

IMOGENE. No, you didn't.

MAUDE. Yeah...you're right.

EADDY. IT WAS AN ACCIDENT! I didn't mean to shoot the captain. *(Beat.)* I meant to shoot *you* Beatrice!

(EVERYONE *gasps as* EADDY *pulls out a gun and points it at* BEATRICE.)

STEVEN. Where are all these guns comin' from? The security on this ship sucks. I have got to find a new job.

BEATRICE. What? Why Eaddy? Why would you –

EADDY. Because you dragged me into this world of sin and debauchery...*hiccup*...and you ruined my life.

      (EADDY takes a step toward BEATRICE. SAM, IMOGENE & MAUDE all gasp and scream.)

ROCKSTONE. Hey lady...now you don't have to do this...please...put down the weapon.

BEATRICE. What's the big deal? So, ya' got your boobs felt up a little...you're gonna kill me over that?

EADDY. What's the big deal? Really? You have corrupted me...you...you...devil woman!

BEATRICE. Please don't kill me Eaddy... I still haven't slept with Jack Nicholson!!

      (EADDY fires the gun. It is a toy cap gun. BEATRICE jumps around, flailing her arms and screaming as if she has been shot. EADDY begins laughing hysterically.)

EADDY. Ahhhh-hahahaha the look on your face is priceless! This is the best day of my life!!

      (SAM, IMOGENE and MAUDE all squint and look closer at the gun.)

MAUDE. Wait –

SAM. Is that –

IMOGENE. – a cap gun?

BEATRICE. What the hell?

      (CAPTAIN STERLING bursts through the stage curtain. He has a fake bloody bullet hole on his forehead. BEATRICE, IMOGENE, MAUDE and SAM scream.)

EADDY. OK...this was the greatest time of my life...*hiccup*...thank you Captain Sterling.

CAPTAIN. No...thank *you* Ms. Clayton...and thank you everyone...thank you so much for participating in

Regency Cruise Lines first ever murder mystery evening. You have all made it a great success.

BEATRICE. A great success? Are you friggin' kidding me with this shit?

MAUDE. I don't understand...you're not dead. Why aren't you dead?

IMOGENE. I'm so confused.

>*(**ROCKSTONE** and **STEVEN** take hands with the **CAPTAIN** and take a bow as the others look around bewildered and lightly clap.)*

CAPTAIN. Let's give an extra round of applause to Miss Tequila Mockingbird...and Melvin Trickle who played our detective. *(Beat.)* By the way Melvin...they need you back in the kitchen...the dirty dishes are piling up.

>*(**ROCKSTONE** scowls and exits through the curtains.)*

BEATRICE. Eaddy! You...are a pig from hell! I could have had a heart attack –

EADDY. *(Baby Jane.)* But ya' didn't Beatrice...ya' didn't have a heart attack...*hiccup*...so get over it.

STEVEN. Now...don't fight ladies...it was all in good fun.

MAUDE. I knew what was going on all along.

SAM. No you didn't.

MAUDE. Yeah...ok...whatever.

IMOGENE. How on earth did you pull this off Eaddy?

BEATRICE. AND WHY EADDY...WHY?

EADDY. Well actually...it wasn't even my idea.

STEVEN. We've been planning to do one of these murder mystery nights for a while now.

CAPTAIN. I mentioned it to Ms. Clayton during breakfast yesterday –

EADDY. – and so I cooked this up with them to get you back for all those times you really *ticked* me off...

BEATRICE. What are you talking about?

EADDY. Well...like that time you kidnapped me and drove me to that gay men's nude beach resort in Key West... and the time you made me go to that topless biker bar... *hiccup*...and the time you put Ex-lax in my brownies just for a laugh...and the time you –

BEATRICE. OK! OK I GET IT! Have another drink...have two!

EADDY. *(Toast.)* Cheers!

MAUDE. Well...I'll join ya' Eaddy...I guess that's all the fun I'll be having tonight...now that my date with Herbert is off.

EADDY. *(Angry.)* HERBERT! He is the devil...*hiccup*!

STEVEN. I'm sorry...who's Herbert?

BEATRICE. Some low life Lothario that has been hustling all of us...trying to pick us up. *(Catty.)* Actually...he was successful with a couple of the more *desperate* ones. I suspect he may have stolen some of our jewelry too.

CAPTAIN. Really? One of our passengers? We've had several reports today of missing jewelry from some of the other single ladies on the ship.

MAUDE. I KNEW IT!

EVERYONE. NO YOU DIDN'T!

EADDY. Dear Lord...*hiccup*...please help me as I try to –

IMOGENE. Not now Eaddy!

CAPTAIN. I will have the ship's security locate this man and do a search of his cabin at once.

(The **CAPTAIN** *pulls out his radio and turns to exit.)*

BEATRICE. No wait Captain...I have a much...*much* better idea.

EADDY. Oh no...no no no...not one of *your* ideas!

BEATRICE. Steven –

STEVEN. Yes darlin'?

BEATRICE. How would you like to make a quick fifty bucks?

STEVEN. *(Appalled.)* I am *not* that kind of girl...hee hee... what do you have in mind miss lady?

(**EVERYONE** *looks at* **BEATRICE** *puzzled.)*

BEATRICE. OK everybody...listen...here's what we're gonna do –

(**EVERYONE** *gathers around* **BEATRICE** *and leans in.)*

(Blackout.)

Scene Two

(**HORACE** *and* **EDNA** *shuffle in from stage right in their evening wear.* **HORACE** *still has his dinner napkin tucked into his collar.*)

EDNA. Horace Bumpus...it was your own fault.

HORACE. *I said* I don't want to talk about it.

EDNA. What?

HORACE. I DON'T WANT TO TALK ABOUT IT EDNA!

EDNA. If I've told you once... I've told you a hundred times...NEVER...take a sleeping pill and a laxative on the same night!

HORACE. Could you say that a little LOUDER?

EDNA. What?

HORACE. I DON'T THINK THEY HEARD YOU DOWN IN THE BOILER ROOM!

EDNA. WHAT? SPEAK UP HORACE!

HORACE. NEVERMIND!

EDNA. Why are you so ornery? When we got married...you said you would love me forever.

HORACE. Well...I didn't realize you would live this long!

EDNA. WHAT?

HORACE. NEVERMIND!

EDNA. Horace Bumpus...we have been married for sixty-four years and you don't ever say you love me anymore.

HORACE. I told you once Edna...if anything changes... I'll let you know.

EDNA. WHAT.

HORACE. I SAID I LOVE YOU EDNA!

EDNA. Well, you don't act like it.

HORACE. What are you talking about?

EDNA. You used to be romantic.

HORACE. Romantic? What are you jabberin' on about Edna?

EDNA. Well...for one thing...you used to hold my hand.

> (**HORACE** *grunts and rolls his eyes...then takes* **EDNA***'s hand as they stroll.*)

HORACE. THERE...ARE YOU HAPPY NOW?

EDNA. Yes...well...

HORACE. WELL, WHAT?

EDNA. Well...you also used to kiss me.

> (**HORACE** *again grunts and rolls his eyes... then kisses* **EDNA***'s cheek.*)

HORACE. I LOVE YOU OLD GAL!

> (**EDNA** *gets a mischievous look on her face and then looks around.*)

EDNA. You know Horace...you also used to nibble on my neck.

> (**HORACE** *growls and starts to storm off.*)

HORACE. Dammitt...come on then...let's go!

EDNA. Where are we going?

HORACE. BACK TO OUR CABIN! I HAVE TO GLUE MY TEETH BACK IN!

> (*Blackout.*)

Scene Three

(One hour later. Romantic music and the soft sound of a boat horn. **STEVEN** as Miss Tequila Mockingbird stands at the rail of the ship. A sign on the rail indicates this is The Lido Deck. A life preserver with the name of the ship hangs on the railing. **STEVEN** is looking off into the distance and fanning himself dramatically. His acting is terrible.)*

STEVEN. Oh me...oh my...I am so lonely. If only my Prince Charming would ride up on his white stallion and sweep me off my feet...my big...tired...aching feet. Fiddle dee dee...what is a lonely girl to do?

*(Enter **HERBERT** ...carrying two glasses of champagne.)*

HERBERT. Hello there...I hope I'm not disturbing you. But I couldn't help but notice you were here alone. Are you waiting for your husband?

*(**STEVEN** giggles girlishly behind the fan.)*

Perhaps a boyfriend...or secret lover?

STEVEN. I'm sorry...are you talking...to me?

HERBERT. Yes, I am...beautiful lady –

*(**STEVEN** giggles and then grabs a glass of the champagne...chugs it back...then burps.)*

STEVEN. Beautiful lady? Are you talking to me?

---

* A license to produce *Four Old Broads On The High Seas* does not include a performance license for any third-party or copyrighted music. Licensees should create an original composition or use music in the public domain. For further information, please see the Music and Third-Party Materials Use Note on page iii.

HERBERT. I...uh...I hope I'm not disturbing you.

STEVEN. Oh no...not at all...I was just standing here hoping to meet a handsome man.

HERBERT. Oh really...well...look no further madame.

STEVEN. *(Aside.)* Actually... I said handsome...not hideous.

(**HERBERT** *does not quite hear* **STEVEN.***)*

HERBERT. I'm sorry...what?

STEVEN. Oh nothing...go on...you were saying?

HERBERT. Well, madame...my name is Herbert...Herbert Carnegie.

STEVEN. Carnegie? As in Carnegie Hall New York Carnegie?

HERBERT. Yes...well...it's just a name...and I certainly don't want you to feel intimidated.

> (**STEVEN** *giggles as* **HERBERT** *grandly takes and kisses his hand...which has a large sparkly ring on it.* **HERBERT** *is mesmerized with the ring.)*

My...what a big ring...I mean...hands you have.

STEVEN. All the better to choke you with my dear –

HERBERT. I'm sorry...what?

STEVEN. Oh nothing...it's so nice to make your acquaintance. I'm Barbra...uh...Barbra Monroe.

HERBERT. What a beautiful name. Well...I hope I'm not coming on too strong...but I find you very attractive... and I would love to have dinner with you tonight. I have a beautiful suite on The Promenade Deck...we can have dinner on my private veranda...and get to know each other better.

STEVEN. OH...why wait? I think we both know what we want.

HERBERT. Oh well I –

> (**STEVEN** *pulls* **HERBERT** *in and plants a big kiss on his lips as* **HERBERT** *flails around.* **STEVEN** *delivers his next line in his deepest voice.*)

STEVEN. WOW...you're a terrible kisser.

> (**HERBERT** *registers horror and steps back.*)

HERBERT. Wait...you're...you're...a...a...you're –

STEVEN. A A A A what? What am I...spit it out...are you trying to say the word man? Yes...I'm a man!

> (**STEVEN** *rips his wig off.*)

HERBERT. Ahhh... I don't understand...wait...what?

> (**BEATRICE** *enters nonchalantly filing her nails.*)

BEATRICE. HE SAID...HE'S A MAN! Are you deaf?

> (**BEATRICE** *looks at* **STEVEN** *and they rolls their eyes.*)

STEVEN. I mean...I thought I was very clear.

BEATRICE. *(Calling out.)* OK LADIES...HE'S ALL YOURS!

> (**BEATRICE** *resumes filing her nails as she watches the action unfold.* **STEVEN** *grabs* **HERBERT**'s *champagne and joins* **BEATRICE** *...both laughing as* **EADDY** *and* **MAUDE** *rush on and start whacking* **HERBERT** *with their purses.* **HERBERT** *cries out in pain.*)

HERBERT. HOLY CRAP!

MAUDE.	EADDY.
Where's my bracelet Herbert?	Vengeance is mine!
You told me I was beautiful...asshole!	I let you touch my ninnies!

BEATRICE. Whack him again for me girls...whack him *real* good.

EADDY. Let's throw him overboard!

MAUDE. Yeah!

>*(**EADDY** and **MAUDE** begin to drag **HERBERT** off, but he breaks away and runs back to **STEVEN** and **BEATRICE**.)*

HERBERT. Help! Please help me...they're crazy!

STEVEN. Get off me ya' loser...you'll wrinkle my gown.

MAUDE. Come on Eaddy...let's show him how crazy we really are –

>*(**MAUDE** and **EADDY** grab **HERBERT** and continue whacking him with their purses as **CAPTAIN STERLING** enters.)*

CAPTAIN. I must admit I was a worried about this little plan of yours...but it looks like you have it all under control.

>*(**BEATRICE** gives **STEVEN** a wad of cash.)*

BEATRICE. Here ya' are sweetie...good job...best fifty dollars I ever spent...threw in little extra for ya' too.

STEVEN. OK girls...I've earned my money... I've gotta get out of this girdle. *(Beat.)* Bye bye darlin'...enjoy prison... there's a lot of men in there to kiss! Let's go girl... I need a drink.

BEATRICE. First round is on me.

(*STEVEN and* **BEATRICE** *exit laughing.*)

EADDY. Let's throw him overboard!

MAUDE. Yeah!

(**EADDY** *whacks him again and she and* **MAUDE** *begin to try and hoist him over the rail. The* **CAPTAIN** *stops them.*)

CAPTAIN. OK ladies...I think that's enough.

HERBERT. Please just take me to jail. Pleeeease –

CAPTAIN. We searched your cabin Mr. Rockefeller Vanderbilt Ashcroft Biltmore...and found all the missing jewelry...*and* your passport.

HERBERT. Dammitt!

CAPTAIN. It turns out that Herbert's real name is...Eugene Wiener

HERBERT. IT'S PRONOUNCED WHINER!

EADDY. Oh, I think WIENER is the perfect name for you.

MAUDE. Hit him again Eaddy! Hit the little wiener!

HERBERT. Please just take me to jail... I'll confess to anything.

CAPTAIN. No...I think I'll just leave you here for a few more minutes. Besides...there are a few other ladies that would like to have a word with you too.

(*He calls out to "the other ladies".*)

OK ladies...you can come out now.

(*We hear an angry mob approaching.*)

HERBERT. OTHER LADIES?! No...NO PLEASE.

(**HERBERT** *breaks away and grabs the life preserver from the railing as he runs away* *into the darkness. The* **CAPTAIN** *speaks into his radio as he stares off into the distance.)*

CAPTAIN. Attention all security personnel...Wiener on the run...I repeat...Weiner on the run...I need all available security personnel to The Lido Deck...over –

(We hear **HERBERT** *scream as he jumps overboard...followed by a big splash.)*

Wait...no...make that...Weiner overboard...I repeat... Weiner overboard...all rescue personnel on standby to launch...over –

(The **CAPTAIN** *races off as* **MAUDE** *and* **EADDY** *stare off into the distance.)*

MAUDE. Well Eaddy...I believe our work here is done.

(They laugh.)

(Blackout.)

Scene Four

(The next day in The Starlight Cabaret. A sign on an easel by the entrance, reads CLOSED FOR PRIVATE EVENT. A few wedding decorations and a wedding cake have been added to the room. A banner has been hung across the mylar curtain which reads "HAPPY WEDDING DAY SAM AND IMOGENE." **MELVIN** *stands at the bar arranging champagne glasses. He wears a Devil Halloween costume for the costume party.* **BEATRICE** *enters from stage left. She wears a cone bra, blonde ponytail, headset microphone and corset with garters. She carries a small wedding bouquet and a veil. She crosses to the bar.)*

BEATRICE. Hey...where's the party? Let's get into the groove... I've got places to go and people to see. *(Then.)* Where is everybody?

*(**MELVIN** pours a glass of whiskey and gives it to **BEATRICE**.)*

MELVIN. I haven't seen any of your friends yet.

BEATRICE. I cannot believe they decided to get married before the costume party!

MELVIN. Oh, I think it's kinda fun...we've never done a –

BEATRICE. Oh, who cares what *you* think. I'm still mad at you...fake Columbo.

MELVIN. Sorry ma'am...it was my job...I'm tryin' to get out of the kitchen washing dishes –

BEATRICE. I'm sorry...I didn't mean that... I've just been in a bad mood...most of my life.

MELVIN. *(Speechless.)* Oh ok...um...yeah –

(**SAM** *and* **IMOGENE** *enter from stage right.*
IMOGENE *is dressed as a 1950's Pink Lady
and* **SAM** *is dressed as a T-Bird...complete
with wigs and glasses. They are holding
hands and are very happy.*)

BEATRICE. Well, it's about time...look who it is...the
blushing bride and her crusty old fart. Don't y'all just
look...too precious for words.

(**BEATRICE** *turns away and pretends to gag
herself.*)

IMOGENE. Thank you Beatrice...and don't you just look...
cheap and trashy...as always.

SAM. Where's the rest of the gang?

BEATRICE. Who knows? But they need to haul their butts
down here...'cause I am not waiting forever... I've got
places to go –

IMOGENE. – and people to hump?

SAM. Ladies...play nice now.

IMOGENE. Oh, she knows I love her...don't ya'...ya' old
bimbo?

BEATRICE. Of course, I do...ya' old toothless hag.

MELVIN. Can I get anything for anyone?

BEATRICE. Yes please...Mel Gibson shirtless...holding a
Piña Colada...make it a double –

MELVIN. I'm sorry...what?

(**EADDY** *enters. She is dressed as a Nun and
wears dark sunglasses. She is clearly hung
over.*)

BEATRICE. Ah look...it's Sister Mary Holier Than Thou
Supreme.

EADDY. Bite me... Maria Von Trashy.

BEATRICE. OOO...someone is in a mood today.

EADDY. *(Moaning.)* The hills are alive...with the sound of pounding in my head –

IMOGENE. You look like hell!

EADDY. Thank you Beatty...you always know *just* what to say –

SAM. How much champagne did you drink last night Eaddy?

EADDY. All of it...definitely *all* of it –

MELVIN. At last count...she drank three.

BEATRICE. *Three* glasses...wow. Eaddy...you –

MELVIN. No...three *bottles*.

BEATRICE. THREE BOTTLES!? Boy...when you let loose... *you let loose*...you're gonna have to say *A WHOLE LOT* of Hail Mary's this time Sister Betty Ford.

EADDY. Dear Lord...give me strength.

> *(***EADDY*** *staggers to a table, plops down in a chair and puts her head down.* ***BEATRICE*** *goes to the bar and grabs her drink and takes it to* ***EADDY****.)*

BEATRICE. Here Eaddy...drink this...you'll feel better.

> *(***EADDY*** *raises her head, takes the glass and takes a big gulp and starts gagging.)*

EADDY. Aaack...what is this?

BEATRICE. Hair of the dog.

EADDY. *(Coughing.)* I am going to kill you!

IMOGENE. So...uh...Beatrice...is that my veil?

BEATRICE. Yes...and your flowers. C'mon...let's go to the bathroom and finish getting you ready. Eaddy...when I get back... I expect a smile on that face...or I'll put one on it myself!

(**BEATRICE** *scowls at* **EADDY**...*grabs the flowers and veil, then exits right.* **IMOGENE** *peck kisses* **SAM** *and follows.*)

MELVIN. Excuse me, I need to make sure everything is ready for the costume party. They're letting everyone else in as soon as the wedding is over. I'll be back in five. Help yourself to the bar...well...except for the nun...she needs a break.

(**MELVIN** *exits left.* **EADDY** *begins sobbing.*)

SAM. Eaddy...can I get you anything? Aspirin? Water? *(Beat.)* An Exorcist?

EADDY. I can't believe I did this!

SAM. DID what...had a little fun?

EADDY. Let myself be such a...a sinner! I am going straight to hell in a handbasket –

(**SAM** *crosses to* **EADDY** *to comfort her.*)

SAM. Well...then move over and make room... I guess I'm going with ya'... *(Then.)* Eaddy...it's ok –

EADDY. Sam...I let a man...well...you know...and then I drank alcohol...*a lot* of alcohol –

(**SAM** *looks at* **EADDY** *for a moment then gently touches her shoulder.*)

SAM. Eaddy...I don't want to *get into your personal business (Beat.)* but...hmmm...how can I say this nicely? *(Beat.)* You need to remove that stick from your hiney...pronto!

EADDY. *(Gasps.)* I beg your pardon?

SAM. You are entirely too uptight.

EADDY. Sam Smith...I can't believe –

SAM. Eaddy...it's my wedding day and you are dragging around here acting like you've...uh...*entertained*...every man this side of the Mason-Dixon.

EADDY. Well, I wouldn't expect a man to understand... especially one with your reputation.

SAM. My reputation? *(Beat.)* OOOO...you mean all that talk about me canoodling with all the ladies at Magnolia Place?

EADDY. Yes...I –

SAM. Eaddy...I wouldn't believe everything I hear...if I were you.

EADDY. What do you mean?

SAM. I mean...my reputation as a Casanova might be...a bit...you know...inflated.

EADDY. What are you saying?

SAM. I'm saying...that...I uh...*might* have...you know... started the rumors myself...

EADDY. WHAT?

SAM. Yeah...well...I wanted to make all the other guys jealous...and have a little fun.

EADDY. SO...what does that have to do with me?

SAM. Eaddy...look...all I'm saying is...it's ok to have a little *fun* in your golden years...you've earned it. I mean...I know I certainly have...and *who cares* what everyone else thinks? You only get one ride on this crazy merry-go-round. So, live a little...and give yourself a break –

EADDY. So, you think it's ok to meet a man and do a little... smoochin'?

SAM. No *(Beat.)* I think it's ok to meet a man and do a lot of smoochin'...and anything else you want to do...in moderation of course.

EADDY. Really?

SAM. Sure...I mean...you don't have to go overboard and be completely indiscriminate –

EADDY. Like Beatrice?

SAM. Hey now...no judgement...she's just being herself... and having a little fun. Actually, you could probably learn a little something from her.

EADDY. I don't think I am ready for that level of fun... I might have a heart attack.

SAM. Just be yourself Eaddy...and don't be afraid to live a little. You never know...you might meet someone and fall in love...like I did with my beautiful Imogene. You don't have to sit around knitting and playing Bingo the rest of your life.

EADDY. Thank you Sam...thank you for that –

>*(**MAUDE** enters stage left dressed as a Playboy bunny in a satin sweetheart one piece suit with tall satin ears, tuxedo cuffs and collar, and a bunny tail. She carries two bridesmaid bouquets, a basket filled with rose petals and a camera.)*

MAUDE. OK...I guess I am as ready as I am gonna be –

EADDY. Sweet Mary and Joseph –

SAM. – and all the saints in heaven.

EADDY. What exactly are you wearing Maude?

>*(**MAUDE** turn upstage and strikes a pose... then turns back and looks over her right shoulder.)*

MAUDE. *(Sexy.)* I'm your bunny waitress Maude...can I take your order?

EADDY. Yes...please...I *order you* to immediately go and change clothes.

> (**BEATRICE** *and* **IMOGENE** *enter stage right.* **IMOGENE** *is now wearing her veil and carries her bouquet. She crosses and meets* **SAM** *at the stage.* **BEATRICE** *crosses to* **MAUDE** *and gets a bouquet.)*

MAUDE. Me? What about ole' cone boobs over there?

EADDY. *(Stern.)* Well, I think you are both going to –

> (**SAM** *holds out his hand to get* **EADDY** *to hold her tongue.)*

BEATRICE.   MAUDE.
Going to where Eaddy?   Where are we going?

SAM. Eaddy? I think they both look very nice...don't you?

EADDY. Um...yes...yes...you both look like you're *going* to *(Beat.)* have *fun* tonight...lots of fun –

MAUDE. Oh...well thank you Eaddy... NOW ...let's get this shindig going...I've got a date for the costume party.

> (**MAUDE** *gives* **EADDY** *a bouquet.)*

EADDY. A date?

BEATRICE. So, who's the lucky guy Maude...Elmer Fudd?

> (**BEATRICE** *laughs hysterically but stops abruptly as* **CAPTAIN STERLING** *enters. He is dressed as Hugh Hefner in black silk pajamas and a red and black brocade smoking jacket. He wears his captain's hat and carries a prop Playboy Magazine. He crosses to* **MAUDE** *and kisses her cheek.)*

CAPTAIN. Hello beautiful.

> (**EVERYONE** *is stunned...particularly* **BEATRICE,** *who's mouth falls open.*)

MAUDE. *(Snarky.)* You better close your mouth Beatrice... are you trying to catch flies?

IMOGENE. Well...don't you two make a...um...cute couple?

SAM. Not as cute as us of course.

BEATRICE. A couple?

MAUDE. Here Sam...please take our picture.

> (**MAUDE** *gives* **SAM** *the camera. She strikes a funny pose by the* **CAPTAIN.**)

CAPTAIN. I hope you're not upset Ms. Shelton...I wanted to –

BEATRICE. *(Flustered.)* I...uh...yes...I mean no...I mean... I thought...I mean...is *that* what you're wearing to marry Sam and Imogene.

CAPTAIN. Oh...no...I'm not –

IMOGENE. Oh...that' right...we completely forgot to tell y'all –

BEATRICE. Forgot to tell us what?

SAM. We're gettin' married by Dolly!

> (**STEVEN** *enters through the mylar curtains. He is dressed as a very busty Dolly Parton.* **MAUDE** *grabs her camera and takes a picture.*)

EADDY. What?

STEVEN. Hey y'all...it costs a lot of money to look this cheap!

CAPTAIN. Steven is also an ordained minister...and sometimes does little ceremonies for us here on the ship. *(Stink eye.)* However...he *is* currently on probation –

BEATRICE. Probation?

STEVEN. Well...you see...last month this cute little couple from Picayune, Mississippi...wanted to get married by me, as Liza Minelli...but...I got a little carried away with my high kicks during my *New York, New York* number and accidentally kicked out the groom's teeth.

IMOGENE. Oh my –

STEVEN. It was dentures...he just popped 'em back in.

MAUDE. Oh, I just love this...it's so romantic...it's even better than getting married by Elvis in Las Vegas.

> (**MAUDE** *snaps a picture of* **BEATRICE** *and* **EADDY.** *The flash causes* **EADDY** *to moan and cover her eyes.* **MELVIN** *enters with a boom box and crosses to the bar.)*

SAM. OK everybody...let's do this...we aren't gettin' any younger.

CAPTAIN. Well...someone is impatient.

SAM.	IMOGENE.
Chop chop.	Time's a wastin'

STEVEN. Everyone please take your places.

> (**IMOGENE, MAUDE, BEATRICE** *and* **EADDY** *all cross right and line up.* **MAUDE** *has the basket of petals.* **SAM** *takes his place at the altar.* **CAPTAIN STERLING** *stands stage left of the altar.* **MELVIN** *turns on the boom box and a 1950's Doo-Wop Wedding song plays as* **MAUDE,** *followed by* **BEATRICE, EADDY** *and*

then **IMOGENE** *cross to the altar**. **MAUDE** *joyfully tosses petals in the air.* **EVERYONE** *lines up at the altar.* **IMOGENE** *meets* **SAM** *in the center, and they join hands.* **MAUDE** *puts down her basket and takes a picture. The flash blinds* **SAM** *and* **IMOGENE**. **BEATRICE** *snatches the camera from* **MAUDE**.*)*

BEATRICE. ENOUGH with the camera Maude!

(**EVERYONE** *settles.* **MELVIN** *stops the music.*)

STEVEN. Dear Friends...we are gathered here today to join this adorable couple in Holy matrimony.

IMOGENE. Oh, my word...we are really doing this!

SAM. Imogene...you're the one that I want.

(**IMOGENE** *strikes a sexy pose.*)

IMOGENE. Tell me about it...STUD!

(**IMOGENE** *and* **SAM** *start to kiss...but* **STEVEN** *stops them.*)

STEVEN. Hey y'all...we are not to that part yet.

(**SAM** *leans over and whispers into* **STEVEN**'s *ear.*)

Oh...OK...I see...ok...well...the bride and groom have asked that we make this ceremony snappy...so I will just ask...Imogene Fletcher...do you take this man, Samuel Thomas Smith, to be your lawfully wedded husband?

IMOGENE. *(Giggle.)* I do.

---

* A license to produce *Four Old Broads On The High Seas* does not include a performance license for any third-party or copyrighted music. Licensees should create an original composition or use music in the public domain. For further information, please see the Music and Third-Party Materials Use Note on page iii.

STEVEN. Sam Smith...do you take this woman, Imogene Joyce Fletcher to be your lawfully wedded wife?

SAM. You bet I do!

MAUDE. *(Tearful.)* Oh...this is so beautiful!

STEVEN. OK then...I guess that's it y'all. By the power vested in me...by The Jim and Tammy Faye Bakker Mail Order Ordainment Program...I now pronounce you...husband and wife! *(Beat.)* You may *now* kiss the bride!

>   (**SAM** *and* **IMOGENE** *have a little kiss and stare into each other's eyes.*)

CAPTAIN. Well then...congratulations you two! I suppose I should get ready for the party... I'll give you a few minutes before I let the other guests in. *(Then to* **MAUDE.***)* And I'll see *you* a little later beautiful lady.

MAUDE. You know it handsome!

>   (**BEATRICE** *grimaces and rolls her eyes.* **MELVIN** *crosses to the easel and removes the PRIVATE EVENT sign, revealing a sign advertising the costume party. He exits with the PRIVATE EVENT sign.*)

BEATRICE. Well...thank God that's over.

STEVEN. All right then...if you'll excuse me...I need to go change my costume. I'm performing later as Cher during the costume party. *(He does a Cher impression.)* Congratulations you two.

>   (**STEVEN** *exits center.* **IMOGENE** *gives a big fake yawn.*)

IMOGENE. Well goodness y'all...I am just *pooped*...getting married is *exhausting*. I think I'm going to skip the costume party... I need to go lie down now. How about you Sam?

(**SAM** *gives a big fake yawn.*)

SAM. Oh...uh...yeah...me too...I'm pretty tired after all this.

MAUDE. *(Singsong.)*
WE KNOW WHAT YOU'RE GONNA DOO-OO!

EADDY. Oh Maude...stop!

BEATRICE. I wouldn't plan on any action Sam... Imogene dumped all your Viagra overboard when she was mad at you.

SAM. Oh...that's ok...I don't really need it... I just take it at night to help keep me from rolling out of the bed.

IMOGENE. Bye y'all...if the boat is a rockin'...don't come a knockin'!

> (**SAM** *and* **IMOGENE** *exit stage left.* **IMOGENE** *tosses her bouquet over her shoulder and* **BEATRICE** *catches it and then immediately throws it across the room.*)

BEATRICE. Hell will sooner freeze over.

MAUDE. I'll take it... I'll take it –

> (**MAUDE** *runs for the bouquet.*)

EADDY. Well...with this nasty hangover...I don't think I want to be around a whole bunch of over the hill alcoholics in costumes.

MAUDE. You're not going to stay for the party?

EADDY. No...actually...I was thinking of going *(Beat.)* up to the topless sundeck.

BEATRICE & MAUDE. What?!

EADDY. What? I can't have a little fun?

> (**BEATRICE** *looks up to the ceiling, alarmed... causing* **MAUDE** *to do the same.*)

MAUDE. What? What? What are you looking at?

BEATRICE. I was just looking for the bolt of lightning that is going to strike us at any minute.

MAUDE. *(Gasp.)* The what?

BEATRICE. The lighting from the sky. Surely if the saintly Ms. Eaddy Mae Clayton is willing to have a little fun on the topless sun deck...the world is coming to an end.

EADDY. OK...OK...I get it...you don't need to carry on Beatty.

MAUDE. Well...if Eaddy is goin'...then I suppose I'll go too.

EADDY. What about your...date?

MAUDE. Oh...he'll wait...I'd rather hang out with my girls... that *was* the whole reason for this trip...and besides...I *can't* miss a topless nun...and don't think for a second that I'm not taking pictures for my scrapbook.

> **(MAUDE** *snatches the camera back from* **BEATRICE.**)

BEATRICE. Well...I guess if you're both going... I better go with you.

EADDY. Oh really? I though you would be staking out your claim on all the eligible old fogies. Ya' know...I hear there are at least three that have all their own teeth... and one that still drives at night.

BEATRICE. *(Whatever.)* Eh...we still have five days left –

EADDY. Oh yeah...then you still have plenty of time to be a bimbo.

BEATRICE. Look who's talkin'...Miss Touch My Ninnies 1995.

EADDY. RUDE!

BEATRICE. PRUDE!

EADDY. WITCH!

BEATRICE. BITCH!

(**EADDY** *and* **BEATRICE** *giggle and embrace.*)

MAUDE. HEY...what am I...chopped liver?

EADDY. Oh Maude...get over here.

(*They all embrace in a big ball of love.* **MAUDE** *holds the camera up and takes the trio's picture.*)

MAUDE. OK Eaddy...if you are really gonna go topless... I'll do it too.

BEATRICE. Oh, that oughta be special...we'll need to see if they have a forklift for those knockers.

MAUDE. Beatrice...please shut your mouth when you're talkin' to me.

EADDY. OK enough...no squabblin' tonight y'all...tonight is special...so sing with me –

MAUDE. Sing?

BEATRICE. Sing what?

(**EADDY** *begins to sing.*)

EADDY.
DOOOOOO YOOOOUR...BOOBS HANG LOW...DO THEY WOBBLE TO AND FRO...

(*Beat.*)

(**MAUDE** *and* **BEATRICE** *join in and start a conga line...dancing around and then off stage left.* **MAUDE** *is the caboose.*)

MAUDE, BEATRICE & EADDY. Can you tie 'em in a knot... can you tie 'em in a bow...

EADDY. Can you throw 'em over your shoulder...like a big ole' bag of boulders...

MAUDE, BEATRICE & EADDY. ...do your booooobs hang low?

MAUDE. ONE MORE VERSE!

MAUDE, BEATRICE & EADDY. Do your boobs hang low... Do they wobble to and fro...Can you tie 'em in a knot...can you tie 'em in a bow...

(The ladies head for the stage left door.)

EADDY. Do they get real sore...

BEATRICE. ...when you drag 'em on the floor...

MAUDE, BEATRICE & EADDY. ...do your boooooooobs... haaaaaang...looooowwwww?

*(**MAUDE** kicks back her leg with a smile and a wink as she exits.)*

MAUDE. Cha Cha Cha.

(Blackout.)

End Play

www.ingramcontent.com/pod-product-compliance
Lightning Source LLC
Chambersburg PA
CBHW070349120726
47909CB00008B/2768